Divide and Conquer

Carrie Ryan

D0001953

SCHOLASTIC INC.

For my nephews, Ryan and Alex
There are so many worlds to explore ahead of you
—C.R.

Copyright © 2012 by Scholastic Inc., *Publishers since 1920*. All rights
reserved. Published by Scholastic Inc. SCHOLASTIC, INFINITY RING,
and associated logos are trademarks and/or registered trademarks of
Scholastic Inc.

This book is a work of fiction. Names, characters, places, and incidents are
either the product of the author's imagination or are used fictitiously, and
any resemblance to actual persons, living or dead, business establishments,
events, or locales is entirely coincidental.

This book was originally published in hardcover by Scholastic Inc. in 2012.

ISBN 978-0-545-90017-1
10 9 8 7 6 5 4 3 2 1   15 16 17 18 19

Book design by Keirsten Geise
Redcoat: Heyworks Unity Studio © Scholastic Inc.

This edition first printing, August 2015
Printed in the U.S.A.   40

Getting Sacked

SERA OPENED her eyes. She was staring at the exact same wall she'd been facing when she'd closed them just a moment before. Her stomach tightened with anxiety. "That can't be right," she murmured.

She looked down at the Infinity Ring, grasped so hard between her fingers that her knuckles were white. "I know I put in the data correctly." Just a few seconds ago they'd been standing in Paris in 1792, and then she'd felt the still-uncomfortable squeezing of her skin. It was the tightening of time and space around her as she moved from one era to another. And it should have brought her, Dak, and Riq to 885.

Yet here they were, staring at the same stupid wall as before.

"This is so cool!" Her best friend, Dak, stood next to her, running his hands over the uneven stones with a look of rapture on his face. Apparently he hadn't spent enough time admiring it before they'd attempted to warp through time. It was bound to keep him occupied for a while. After all, Dak could get excited by something as boring as a wall simply because it was historical—and here, *everything* was historical.

She turned to Riq. He was the one who she didn't know as well, and she hated the idea of him thinking her incompetent. "Sorry, I'm not sure what went wrong. This should only take a second," she told him, her mind already whirring through the complicated mathematical equations to find the mistake. Riq shrugged, as though ending up in the wrong place and time was something altogether ordinary rather than an absolute catastrophe.

"Really, I think we must be dealing with some sort of hidden variable aspect to the quantum entanglement." As her fingers flew over the Ring's controls, Sera felt herself speaking a bit uncontrollably, explaining in painstaking detail the scientific theories behind the warping of space and time. She tried to force her mouth closed, but she couldn't help it. When she got nervous, she talked.

Riq kept his focus on the wall, a frown furrowing his forehead. "I could have sworn this wasn't there before," he said, his fingers tracing over a series of scratches in the stone.

"Check it out! There must be thousands of them!" Dak had found a series of footholds and managed to climb to the top of the wall. He was staring out beyond it at something in the distance. Then he looked down at Sera, his entire body vibrating with excitement, like the time (was it really only a few days ago?) that the two of them had gone on a class trip to the Smithsonian.

That hadn't turned out well—an earthquake had struck and they were almost crushed by a Viking longship on display. Just thinking about it gave Sera a dawning sense of unease. "Dak, maybe you should get down," she called out. "I'm not sure—"

"Duck!" Riq called out, cutting Sera off.

For a split second Dak looked confused but then he did as he was told, flattening himself against the top of the wall. Just then a storm of rocks and debris came hurtling through the air, raining down around the three of them. The wall shuddered at the impact.

Sera pressed the Infinity Ring to her stomach to protect it as Riq lunged forward, throwing himself on top of her. Now probably wasn't the best time to realize that none of them had showered in several days, and smelled like it.

Then Sera had another realization. If the arrows slicing through the air around her weren't enough of a clue, the moment she actually took in her surroundings all thoughts of quantum entanglement fled her mind. The warp hadn't failed after all.

Where before there'd been the elegant flying buttresses of Notre Dame Cathedral, with its intricately patterned windows, there now sat a dull, plain hulk of a church with thick, bare walls. A palace still occupied the western end of the Île de la Cité, but no longer did it dominate the tip of the island with its impressive turrets and elaborate facades. Everything was different than it had been a minute ago, from the width of the streets to the uneven construction of the buildings to the sounds of men running for cover. Now that she really looked, Sera realized that even the wall Dak had scaled was different. Whereas in 1792 they'd taken refuge against the scrap of an old ruin, now the wall stood strong and sure, rising several yards in the air and securely ringing most of the island.

Leave it to a genius to miss the obvious, Sera thought. *This* definitely *isn't 1792.*

Wave after wave of arrows and rocks pounded into the ground and crashed into nearby buildings. Sera wondered if it would ever end. Somehow, when the three of them had agreed to travel through time fixing the Breaks in history, she hadn't seriously considered the danger they'd be in.

But so far, time travel had offered up one life-threatening peril after another. Starting with the very first trip, when Dak and Sera had warped with Dak's parents to test the brand-new Infinity Ring. They'd ended up in the middle of a Revolutionary War battle, with uniformed men running at them with guns and bayonets at the ready. The group had barely made it out alive — and they'd been separated from Dak's parents in the process.

Sera wasn't ashamed to admit it: She was scared. She and Dak were just eleven years old and Riq wasn't much older — having the fate of the world in their hands felt a bit overwhelming.

When the rubble stopped falling and Riq pulled away, she noticed that he seemed a little shaken, too. At least she wasn't alone.

Of course, then Dak called out, "That was awesome!" from his perch.

"How did you know to tell him to duck?" Sera asked Riq. Whether Dak realized it or not, the warning had probably saved his life.

Riq pointed at the wall. "The picture scratched into the stone—it's a duck. That we would warp into this exact spot and be facing this . . . I figured it might be a message for us somehow, and I didn't want to take the chance of ignoring it."

Sera stepped forward and squinted at the poorly drawn waterfowl. Then she saw something that made her lungs tighten. "It *was* a message for us," she said, tracing her fingers over two numbers: 34 and 88. "This is a code for my name. Thirty-four is the number on the periodic table for the element selenium. Eighty-eight is the number for radium. The abbreviations for them are Se and Ra—*Sera*." She cringed a bit. "I know that makes me sound like a total geek."

"No," Riq responded with a smile. "You're talking to a guy whose idea of a good time is tracing the etymology of obscure words. I think it's pretty cool that you came up with that."

Sera cleared her throat, unsure how to respond. She wasn't used to that kind of compliment. "Anyway, it was always an inside joke I had with Dak, but his parents knew about it, too. Do you think they left it for us? How old is this wall, anyway?"

Just then, Dak leapt the last few feet to the ground, landing between them. "Guys!" His eyes were alight with excitement. "You're not going to believe it. The entire Seine is filled with them for as far as I could see! It's like a huge logjam out there. You can't even see the water. They're everywhere!"

Sera couldn't help smiling. She'd been Dak's best friend for as long as she could remember, and she knew he was waiting for her to ask the inevitable question: "What's everywhere?"

His grin widened. "Vikings! There must be seven hundred ships out there — probably more if you count the barques. Those are the little boats." He explained that last bit to Riq.

The older boy gave Dak a forced smile. "Thanks, got that. Linguist here, remember? My vocabulary is just fine."

Dak ignored him. "This is incredible! There have always been debates about how many boats the Vikings attacked Paris with. Some scholars said they stretched for two leagues but others argued there weren't that many based on the application of operational space in a stationary —"

"Dak, focus." Sera rolled her eyes, but not in a mean way. She was used to putting up with his ramblings about obscure historical details. And to be honest, she kind of liked it because it was so, well . . . so *Dak*.

He glanced between her and Riq. "According to the history books, there are thirty thousand Vikings on the other side of that wall, preparing for the great Siege of Paris!"

Something sank inside Sera, but Riq was the one to

voice what she was feeling. "Did the history books happen to give a date for this sack?"

Dak nodded vigorously. "November 25, 885."

Sera sucked in a long breath. "That's . . . tomorrow," she said.

But Dak wasn't finished yet. "Though some historians put the date at November 24 based on the account of one of the monks inside the fortified city. . . ."

Riq looked at Sera, and his expression matched hers. Before either of them could say anything more there was a great blast of horns from the other side of the wall and the roar of thirty thousand men screaming at once. The ground trembled from the force of so many feet pounding against it as the massive horde of Vikings raced toward the city.

Dak seemed utterly unconcerned. "Huh." His face scrunched up in concentration. "I guess it was the twenty-fourth after all. I can't wait until we get back and I can correct the—"

"Dak!" Sera shouted. "The Vikings are sacking Paris and we're *inside* the city! They're about to attack *us*!"

2

Mathy Stuff

DAK DIDN'T quite understand why Sera was so panicked. After all, there was a wall *and* a river between them and the approaching horde of Vikings. While the Paris of 1792 that they'd just left had sprawled far into the countryside, the Paris they'd arrived in was little more than a fortress on an island in the middle of the Seine River. Sure, the stone wall ringing the island was already about four hundred years old and was crumbling in places, but it still gave them *some* protection.

Besides, if he knew his history (which he always did), the invasion wouldn't really get under way until the leaders of each side met to discuss the terms of Paris's surrender. Unfortunately for the people of Paris, surrendering wouldn't be enough to keep the Vikings from stealing provisions and setting most of the island on fire—it was just how Vikings did things. And, okay, thought Dak, they probably shouldn't stick around for too much of that. But they still had time to explore the area and figure out the Break before getting worried.

Even so, it wouldn't be good to get hit by a random arrow, and he could tell Sera was freaking out, so he let her drag him and Riq to the nearest shelter, an empty house nestled between two bakeries. The air inside smelled of yeast and butter, and dust covered most of the surfaces, causing the spare bits of light sneaking through the cracks in the tile roof to sparkle. The space was narrow, and they wove their way between wooden support pillars toward the deepest recesses of the shelter. Just as they took cover another wave of arrows and rocks flew over the wall, raining down outside.

Thankfully, it looked like everyone else had the same idea as they did and had found someplace safe to hide out. Paris looked like a ghost town. But it didn't sound like one. Even inside their tiny shack, the noise of so many Vikings racing toward the island was tremendously loud. It reminded Dak of going to the biennial SQ games with his parents and the roar of the cheering crowds. Except this crowd was probably more deadly than a couple thousand sports fans.

Now that they were clear of all the falling debris, Sera pulled the SQuare from its satchel. A portable tablet computer given to them by the Hystorians, it was their only remaining connection to the future where, or rather *when*, they'd come from. He noticed her hands shook ever so slightly as she typed out the password to access the files.

"Okay, whiz kid," Riq said to Dak as he leaned against a rough stone wall. "You're the one who's always bragging about your historical prowess. Any idea why we're here and what's going on?"

Dak let a satisfied grin split his face. "Now look who's interested in what I have to say." Dak wondered for a second if he'd really get in all that much trouble if he pushed Riq out into the debris storm. He thought better of it when Sera raised her head from the SQuare and scowled at both of them.

"Keep your voices down," she hissed, though Dak was pretty sure her whisper was louder than her normal tone of voice. "We haven't spoken to anyone here yet, which means our translation devices aren't set for the correct local language."

Before they'd been sent back in time by Hystorians Brint and Mari to fix the Breaks in history, all three of them had been given earpieces and a tiny device to fit over one of their teeth that would translate anything they said. The only catch was that they had to hear someone talk before the device knew which language to use.

"Sorry," Dak mumbled, but he still took the opportunity to smirk at Riq. Riq was the language expert—his parents had even invented the translation tool—and he should have been the one to remind them to stay quiet.

"Oh, for the love of mincemeat," Sera muttered. Apparently she didn't even have to glance up from the SQuare to know Dak and Riq were staring each other down to see who looked away first. (Riq totally forfeited when he turned to look at Sera.)

The SQuare's screen flickered a few times. "Any idea if they had time to upload anything on this Break?" Sera asked Riq. "I hate to think about being cast adrift with no help."

Riq frowned and for once it seemed to Dak like the older boy might admit to not having all the answers. "I think they were able to get most everything on there," he said. "Are the files not showing up?"

Sera shook her head. "Some of it. I guess until we know how many of the files are corrupted, we just have to work with the information we have." Dak came to look over her shoulder as she chose the option for learning more about the third Break.

A few words and a long string of numbers flashed up on the screen.

Leave a message after the beep:
326274827332 744332413373433231 8121523274
7121734374 71322123323382535393

Dak groaned. "What kind of a message are they expecting us to leave?" He was good with words — facts and details, especially historical ones. Numbers just tended to swim in his head unless they were specific dates. In fact, sometimes in math class the only way he could remember his multiplication tables was to attach each set to a series of historical events.

He watched helplessly now as both Sera's and Riq's eyes tracked back and forth across the screen. This was so not how he envisioned the Siege of Paris going. Thirty thousand Vikings nearby and he was stuck inside a bakery with two geeks more interested in mathy stuff.

"It could be a code or a cipher," Riq suggested.

"*Hmmm*," Sera murmured. "I guess it could be a mono-alphabetic substitution cipher—like maybe an affine?"

Even their conversation was boring! While they were engrossed in their boring boringness, Dak began to ease his way to the door. He only wanted to catch a glimpse of what was happening outside, get a feel for what was going on.

Already the ground was littered with stones of all sizes, some larger than his head and a few so big they could have crushed a cow if any had been milling about (thankfully, it appeared none had).

Dak breathed deeply, letting a smile cross his face. For as long as he could remember, he'd been in love with history. He even read most historical accounts in old books rather than on SQuares, because he loved how history smelled.

But now it felt like the words he'd read had always been dry. They'd tried to capture past events, to transport him there in his mind, but as he stood on the Île de la Cité, the Island of Paris, Dak realized that the books had been mere ghosts. Reality was so much cooler. Smellier, too.

Just then, the bombardment stopped, and the cacophony of war horns and shouts from the other side of the wall was replaced with the sound of ringing church bells. Dak watched as a contingent of Vikings started to make their way into the city over a low stone bridge that stretched across the Seine from the north bank of the river.

Dak wanted nothing more than to run forward and get a better look, but Sera already had her hand firm on his shoulder. "Don't even think about it. We have a Hystorian to find. Here, help us figure out what this means."

She held out the SQuare, and Dak read the high-lighted lines:

```
To find the person whom you seek
Upset the clue within:
To lead you to the Hystorian
Find a roofless inn.
```

Dak stared at the words, but he had absolutely no clue what they meant. "This should be Riq's gig—he's the expert on things like this," he said. "I'm just the history buff. And as your guide through all past occurrences, I think our time would be better spent eavesdropping."

He pointed toward a small group of Parisians striding through the inner city. Many of them were priests, with ornately decorated tunics over their cowls. Others were soldiers, their own tunics less ornate and complemented with chain mail.

Dak knew an official welcoming party when he saw one. The priests and soldiers were on their way to meet with the Viking contingent on the bridge, and Dak desperately wanted to be there for that discussion. Although he figured the important stuff wouldn't happen until they'd all gathered in some central location.

"Those are the guys who make decisions around here," Dak said. "The Hystorian is probably one of them, or on his way to wherever they're headed. That's where the history is going to happen, and that's where we need to be!"

"You're forgetting that we don't look like Parisians," Sera argued.

"Well, technically we *are* dressed like Parisians. Just Parisians of another century. We're very fashion forward!" Dak tugged on the ruffles at his wrist and wagged his eyebrows.

"Dak . . ." Sera's tone of voice left no question — she was getting fed up.

Dak put a hand on her arm. He and Sera had known each other for a really long time, since before they could talk, actually, but sometimes he didn't understand her at all. These were real, actual, honest-to-Thor *Vikings*. How could she not want to get closer to them? "Trust me," he said. "Have I steered you wrong before? Besides, I think I know what's about to happen. And it could be crucial to our mission here."

Riq looked up from where he was pawing through a low wooden trunk on the other side of the room.

Dak took a moment to relish their undivided attention before diving in. "The small contingent of Vikings crossing into the city is headed by Siegfried, their leader. Well, I don't know if *leader* is the right word since Viking society wasn't strictly ordered the same as ours. Usually power wasn't quite so concentrated—"

Sera cleared her throat and began tapping her foot.

"Er, right. Anyway, just before the Vikings sack Paris, Siegfried has a little chat with their bishop, Gauzelin, and asks him to hand the city over. The bishop agrees. The Parisians figure everything's cool—so they're pretty surprised when the Vikings attack the next morning."

Riq frowned. "That doesn't seem sportsmanlike," he said.

Dak shrugged. "That's not really what the Vikings are known for. They were more the pillaging-and-plundering kind of folk."

Sera's body appeared to tense a bit at that. "So this Siegfried guy—what happens after he takes Paris?"

Dak felt the same excitement he always did before imparting cool historical details. "He becomes one of the most powerful men in France. See, he ends up settling down in Normandy, the region of France right across the channel from England. It turns out that bit of land is pretty strategically important—it's the perfect launching spot for an invasion of Great Britain in the eleventh century. Siegfried's great-great-great-grandson, Bill Helm the Vanquisher, does just that!"

Sera and Riq stared at him, and it took him a second to realize that they didn't understand the importance of that. He sighed deeply.

"Every modern-day European monarch is descended from Bill Helm the Vanquisher, AKA the dude who conquered England. And, of course, that means . . ." He felt like a teacher trying to pull an obvious conclusion from his students.

"It means every king, every queen — they're all descendants of Siegfried the Viking," Sera answered, her eyes wide.

Riq was the one to say out loud what Dak had already been thinking. "This siege is about more than just Paris. The fate of the whole world is at stake."

Dak nodded. "And with that much power up for grabs, you can bet the SQ is already here."

3

Starting a War

DAK AND Riq stood just outside their shelter to give Sera privacy while she changed. Dak had to grudgingly admit that Riq had done a pretty good job putting together proper outfits from the scraps he'd found in the trunk. Of course, it had taken a bit of doing to figure out what went where. They'd shoved their old shoes into the bottom of their satchel, since nothing screamed *anachronism* more than sneakers.

That still left Dak in a shin-length tunic, and he wasn't sure how he felt about it. It was way too easy to imagine accidentally flashing ninth-century Paris. And he definitely didn't want to think too much about who'd worn these clothes before (and how long it had been since they'd been washed).

At least Riq looked even more ridiculous in his own getup. "You remind me of my grandfather with your socks tied up around your knees like that," Dak quipped.

The older boy smirked at him. "You look like my grandma in your little dress."

Dak couldn't think of a comeback fast enough and resigned himself to scowling. He watched impatiently as more and more Parisians made their way toward a large stone cathedral. His toes curled in his new (old) boots, wanting to join in the throng.

"So, you think this Viking leader Siegfried might be SQ?" Riq asked.

"It seems likely to me," Dak said. "Around the late eighth century the Vikings became pretty aggressive and started taking over a bunch of places, pillaging along the way. Before then they'd more or less stayed up in Norway and Denmark, and no one really knows why they decided to expand their territory. Some historians think it's because, with the Medieval Warm Period, it got easier to head out on the ocean, and others think that available land just became too scarce on the Scandinavian peninsula. Now that I think about it, though, it would make sense that they'd actually be led by SQ going for a big land grab."

Riq nodded. "So what do you think that means for us? Where do you think the Break is?"

Dak had been thinking about this already, his mind whirring over all the possibilities. "Okay, pretend you're Siegfried and you're SQ." He paused and squinted at Riq. "Well, if you were a Viking you'd have a beard and smell less, but moving on."

"You couldn't get a beard if you shaved your head and glued it to your face," Riq muttered.

Dak ignored that. "So you're an evil, stinky, *ugly* SQ

guy with a big army and you're traveling all over the world pushing people around. What are you really after?"

"Power," Sera said as she stepped out to join them. Dak choked on a laugh. Like the rest of them, she was wearing hose fastened at her knees with a scrap of lace, and a tunic draped over a long undershirt and tied around her waist with a belt. From the belt hung a sack with a familiar bulge that could only be the Infinity Ring. A formless brown cape hung from her shoulders to the back of her knees, and what was left of her hair was tucked up into a misshapen wool cap.

"You do a pretty good job passing as a boy." Dak tweaked the cap, making it fall farther over her eyes.

Riq stepped forward and righted it, tucking stray bits of her hair back up under it. "One of these days we'll find a time in history when you can get dressed up nicely," he said.

Dak wanted to groan, but Sera's face lit up at the prospect.

"*Any*way," he interjected. "Sera's right—it's really all about power. That's pretty much what history is: people grabbing power and then losing it to someone else." Which is exactly why Dak loved it so much. Science always seemed like a boring recitation of facts, but history . . . it was all one big adventure story.

"That still doesn't help us fix the Break," Riq said. "And we haven't unraveled the code to figure out what we're supposed to be doing here, or figured out how to find the Hystorian."

"Code, schmode — we've got this." Dak grinned. "Watch and learn, my friend," he said and started strolling toward the church.

The front face of the church loomed over them, towers dotted with arched windows rising on either side of the entrance. Once they were inside, everything was darker, the row of windows close to the ceiling letting in little of the morning's watery light. Already the nave was full of Parisians, many of them spilling into the transepts on either side of the altar.

Thankfully Dak, Sera, and Riq were dressed like everyone else so they didn't stand out so much. Dak used his small size to his advantage, slipping through the crowd toward the front of the church. At times like this it was useful to be young — no one seemed to pay him any attention.

When the contingent of Vikings entered, the crowded church grew so quiet that Dak could hear the rattle of swords in scabbards as the large Danish men strode forward. He was mesmerized. He'd seen depictions of Vikings from tapestries and drawings in his books, but seeing them in person was different. They were huge, with long mustaches braided out to their ears, and beards that fell from their chins.

He'd expected them to look more barbaric — everything he'd ever read about them mentioned their cruelty and filthiness — but these men didn't seem to match that description at all. In fact, they seemed cleaner and better dressed than most of the Parisians.

Their leader, Siegfried, was older than the others. Judging from the lines on his face, he'd probably never once smiled in his life. His cloak was pinned to his right shoulder, which kept his arm free — and even in the cathedral he kept his hand on the hilt of his sword.

Dak was pretty sure that the guy could lop off a head or a leg with one swing, his arms were so thick with muscles. Of course, that didn't stop Dak from edging closer to get a better look. Sera kept hissing at him to stop, but her unease didn't keep her from following as he made his way forward.

Just as they reached the edge of the crowd ringing the altar at the front of the cathedral, an old priest shuffled out of a side room and approached the band of Vikings. He was pretty weighed down with ornate robes that hung from his bony shoulders, and for a moment Dak wasn't sure he'd actually make it across the altar before keeling over. Flanking him were several other clergymen who seemed prepared to catch him if it came to that.

Siegfried stepped forward and spoke first. Dak's earpiece translated every word. "Bishop Gauzelin, have compassion on yourself and on your flock. Allow us the freedom of the city. We will do no harm, and we will see to it that whatever belongs to you shall be strictly protected."

Bishop Gauzelin turned to the priests around him and started to whisper as they debated Siegfried's request.

Dak felt his heart begin to race. "This is it," he whispered to Sera and Riq. "This is where the bishop hands over the city. And did you see what Siegfried is using to pin his cloak?" Dak tilted his head toward the gigantic Viking—whose bronze pin bore the unmistakable insignia of the SQ. "Man, sometimes I hate being right."

"I'm still not sure about this, Dak," Sera fretted. "I think we should figure out what the code from Brint and Mari says before jumping to any conclusions."

It bothered him that Sera had so little faith in him, especially since he'd never been wrong before. Oddly, Riq seemed willing to take his side, which was a rarity in itself. "Do you think that's really all there is to this Break? Keeping that Viking guy from getting into Paris?" Riq asked.

Dak rolled his eyes at Riq's imprecision with historical details. "He's not just 'some guy' and, yeah, I think keeping the bishop from handing over the city is a pretty good start. Siegfried is an agent of the SQ and his power base starts with Paris, so it makes sense to make sure that never happens. We just have to figure out how to do that."

"What if we just—" Riq started to offer.

Dak scoffed and cut him off. "I don't think learning about the origin of some obscure and useless word is what we need right now, and your skills are pretty limited beyond being a linguist."

Riq raised his eyebrows and glanced at Sera, who only shrugged in response. Dak shifted his focus back to the group gathering at the front of the church, trying to figure out how best to intervene.

His thoughts were interrupted by a smarting slap on the back. "Watch and learn, my friend," Riq said over his shoulder as he strode forward. The next thing Dak knew, Riq was leaping onto the dais.

Sera let out an alarmed little squeak as she tried to grab for Riq's tunic but she was too late. Soon enough Riq was approaching the flock of priests. "What's he doing?" she asked.

Dak shrugged; he didn't know, but whatever it was, he wasn't going to be left out. He was just about to climb up after him when Riq stepped between the two groups.

Siegfried looked Riq over dismissively, the furrows on his face deepening. "Who is this boy?"

Riq responded easily and smoothly, showing no fear or hesitation. "Bishop Gauzelin is not as skilled in the Danish tongue as I am and has allowed my assistance as a translator."

Siegfried frowned. One of the large men in his entourage stepped forward, a large red scar across his face puckering as he asked, "And how does one as dark as you come to know the Danish tongue?"

When Riq hesitated to answer the scarred Viking took another step until he was almost towering over the smaller boy. He had the same brutish look about him as the Time Warden they'd run into in Spain. Dak remembered how they'd been caught in Palos de la Frontera during their first Break. The Time Warden overheard them talking just after they'd warped into 1492 and noticed how out of place the three of them looked in their stolen clothes and anachronistic demeanor.

Dak, Sera, and Riq were all too aware of the men and women who'd been trained throughout time to search for anything or anyone suspicious, and a dark-skinned teenager in medieval Paris who knew how to speak French, Latin, and Old Norse certainly qualified as odd. If Siegfried was SQ then it would make sense that one of his men might be a Time Warden, and the Time Warden's only job was to search out time travelers and eliminate them.

They couldn't risk getting caught and right now, getting caught looked likely. Sera gripped Dak's hand hard enough he was pretty sure she'd leave dents in his bones.

"Do something," she urged.

Dak's mind weeded through a myriad of historical details, searching out the best possible excuse for Riq. In the end, it didn't matter because Riq came up with his own solution: the truth. "My father was a scholar," Riq explained. "I speak sixteen languages."

He delivered the explanation with his usual air of smugness and though the scarred Viking opened his mouth as if to press the issue, Siegfried stepped forward, cutting him off. "Ignore Gorm. What is Bishop Gauzelin's response to our request?"

Dak's translator device switched smoothly to French again, and he overheard Gauzelin and Riq speaking back and forth, discussing their response. The bishop was clearly telling Riq to give in to the Viking demands.

Riq nodded in understanding and then turned to Siegfried. "Bishop Gauzelin tells me that Paris has been entrusted to us by the emperor. It is our responsibility to protect it."

Dak's jaw dropped and Sera frowned. "That's not what the bishop said," she whispered.

"Not at all," Dak agreed. He had absolutely no idea what Riq was planning.

Riq continued to talk, falsely translating what the bishop actually said. "If you had been given the duty of defending these walls, and if you instead gave in to the demands of a foreign army, what treatment do you think you would deserve?"

Siegfried laughed, a deep booming sound that echoed off the stone walls. "I would deserve to have my head cut off and thrown to the dogs."

Riq crossed his arms over his chest and Dak was impressed with how imposing he looked among the massive Vikings and the frail priests. "So you understand our position and why we will not yield."

Siegfried stepped forward until he was towering over Riq. In an instant he'd gone from laughter to fury. Sera's grip on Dak's hand tightened, something Dak didn't even think was possible until he felt bones grinding together.

"If you do not bow to my demands," Siegfried growled, "then tomorrow our war machines will destroy you."

Riq grinned. "Bring it on."

Dak almost groaned at the use of such a misdated

phrase but it seemed to have the intended effect of catching Siegfried off guard. The Viking furrowed his brow in confusion before stepping back to join his men. "You've made your choice. Tomorrow face the wrath of Odin's finest warriors." Then they turned and strode from the hall, long cloaks billowing behind them.

The bishop appeared alarmed as he turned to Riq. "What did they say?"

"That we should be ready to fight," Riq answered. It was clear he'd meant for no one beyond their small group to hear the words but even so his voice carried into the crowd. Soon there were strained murmurings that transformed quickly into a startled buzzing as the news made it through the throngs packed into the church. The air hummed with the threat of panic.

Sera finally released Dak's hand, and he grimaced as blood rushed back into his fingertips with a feeling of pins and needles. "What did he just do?" she asked.

Dak stared up at where Riq and the bishop continued to converse. He couldn't help but feel a little jealous of the older boy for taking such a crucial role in changing the course of history. "I'm pretty sure he just started a war."

He watched as Sera's expression morphed from startled to alarmed. But it was envy, not the pending war, that occupied Dak's thoughts. "Riq's totally going to go down in the history books for this, isn't he?"

Another Fan of History

WHEN DAK told Sera there were over thirty thousand Vikings across the river, she hadn't really understood what that meant. Now that she was standing on top of the Grand Châtelet—the huge wooden tower on the mainland guarding the northern bridge to the island city—reality hit her. Hard.

Armored men spread out as far as the eye could see, covering the ground of the mainland's north bank more thickly than blades of grass. Even though dusk was falling fast she could see them milling around, setting up camp and sharpening weapons. In the distance, a large band of them hacked at a massive fallen tree with their axes, honing the tip of it to a point. Another group worked to set up what looked to be a complicated catapult.

It wouldn't be long until they pointed everything they had at the ancient wall ringing the island and let loose with all their might. Sera looked behind her into the city. The wall was old and crumbling, most of it constructed over four hundred years ago by the Romans (according to Dak). She couldn't imagine it holding up for long. Even worse, she'd counted maybe two hundred armed Parisian men during the day. Compared to the legion outside, their force was minuscule.

"You do realize that we're outnumbered, right?" she asked.

Riq glanced up briefly as if calculating. "If each man here personally takes down one hundred and fifty Vikings, we should be fine."

"One hundred and fifty heavily armed, bloodthirsty Vikings," Dak clarified.

Sera stared at the two of them. Neither seemed to grasp the magnitude of the situation. "Oh, no sweat, then."

Sera still felt uneasy at the way Riq had so completely twisted history. No matter how much Dak tried to reassure her that his read on their mission here was the right one, she didn't like how little they knew about what was really going on. She was someone who preferred to amass facts, parse through them, and only then come up with a plan of action that had been considered from every angle.

All of this was happening too fast. The only thing that made Sera less anxious was that at the very least the Parisians now had a fighting chance. Originally, according to Dak, after the bishop handed over the city, the Vikings had waited through the night to lull everyone into a false sense of security before destroying the island in the morning. Now, because of Riq, the Parisians had fair warning and were able to marshal their forces and make a plan for defending themselves.

It was an old plan, actually. A few decades before, King Charles the Bald had ordered that cities along the Seine build low bridges across the river to keep Vikings from being able to sail inland too easily. But the bridges themselves were vulnerable to attack. Towers were supposed to be constructed to protect the bridges.

A lot of cities had started the fortifications but never really finished them. Because of that, there was nothing to keep the agile Viking ships from sailing inland from the sea, and they'd taken advantage of this, sending out raids that had decimated French cities that lay close to the coast.

Paris hadn't finished its fortifications either, and now that the Vikings were set to attack, everyone was pitching in to hurriedly build another level on the tower guarding the north bridge.

I guess procrastination isn't a modern invention, Sera thought darkly. She had suggested finding a quiet spot for the three of them to hole up in while they worked on the encoded information on the SQuare. But before they'd had a chance to sneak off, the bishop had asked Riq personally to help out. That's what he got for jumping in as a translator—he'd become too high profile to fade into the background.

Which meant now Sera was tasked with holding rough-hewn wooden planks while Riq and Dak hammered them into place. It wasn't enough of a distraction from the intimidating view, and her mind drifted back to the danger lurking way too close for comfort.

"I'm still not convinced this can work," she said. "Even with the advance warning, I don't see how so few men will keep the Vikings from taking over."

Dak didn't even stop what he was doing as he responded, "Originally, they didn't. The Vikings creamed the Parisians and pretty much took everything they could get their hands on before claiming the city as their base of power and moving on to conquer more."

Sera glanced at Riq, wondering if Dak's answer was as unsettling for him as it was for her. But Riq seemed engrossed in his task and perfectly willing to ignore both of them. "And you think we've changed all that?"

Dak paused. "Maybe?" That his answer was in the form of a question didn't do much to allay Sera's fears.

"On the plus side," Dak added, "at least now we get to see how a battering ram works." He grinned in his familiar way.

"That's not really something I would put in the *plus* category," Sera muttered.

Dak ignored her. "Speaking of how things work," Dak continued. "As soon as it's dark I'm going to sneak down to the riverbank so I can check out one of the longships. I want to see firsthand if the re-creation at the Smithsonian was accurate."

Sera felt her eyes bulge out of her head. "What?" The word came out almost as a squawk and several heads turned her way, causing her to blush. She lowered her voice and gripped Dak's shoulder. "You're not leaving this tower, Dak Smyth!"

"It'll just be for a second," he argued. "I'll be careful, I promise. Everyone up here is focused on getting the tower fortified, and all the Vikings are wrapped up in their preparations for tomorrow. No one will notice me, honest."

Was Dak crazy? He'd done some reckless things in his life, but Sera couldn't believe he was actually considering leaving the safety of the tower, and alone at that!

"It's out of the question," she told him, and for the briefest flash of a moment she felt the dizzy, uneven sensation that preceded a Remnant. She'd had these feelings before — that her life was somehow missing something that she was brushing right up against — but they'd always happened when she was at home near her barn or when she looked in a mirror.

This time there was something about the phrase she'd just said, her tone of voice and inflection, that felt as though it should have been familiar somehow. She pressed a hand against the wall to steady herself, sweat breaking out along her temples. Dak didn't seem to notice. Or if he did he must have thought she was just upset at his plan to sneak out (which, for the record, she was).

"Listen, Sera," Dak said, setting down his tools and facing her, "when I snuck you into my parents' super-secure workshop and you saw all those white-boards filled with their plans for the Infinity Ring, I didn't try to stop you from working on it. In fact, if I remember correctly I even brought you a nice ham sandwich."

Dak knew exactly how to make Sera feel guilty and, since she was already unsteady in the wake of the passing Remnant, it was difficult for her to come up with a good response. So she settled on "That was different."

"How?"

"Because there weren't thirty thousand Vikings nearby ready to kill you!" Once again Sera's outburst drew the attention of the workers around them, and this time several narrowed their eyes.

Dak stepped forward and put a hand on her arm. Sera knew as soon as he did it that she'd lost the argument.

"I promise I'll be careful," he said. His eyes were pleading and his voice earnest. "You know how important this is to me. My entire life I've lived and breathed history, and now's my chance to actually experience it firsthand. Please, Sera."

Dak was right; he'd let her play around in his parents' lab even though he knew he'd be in huge trouble if they'd found out. He'd taken the risk because of how much it meant to Sera. She sighed dramatically and Dak flashed her an enormous grin.

"One boat, that's it," she told him sternly. "And first, we figure out how to find the Hystorian. That's most important."

Dak's response was a groan. "But those puzzles are so hard! And when we asked about a roofless inn, everyone looked at us like we were crazy!"

She arched an eyebrow, a skill she'd perfected after spending several hours in front of the bathroom mirror. "Then I guess you won't get to see your boat tonight."

Dak buried his head in his hands and Riq slapped him on the back. "Get to work," he said, almost gleeful at Dak's despair.

As it turned out, while Sera was a whiz at calculations and really complicated machines that required using tiny precise instruments, she wasn't all that skilled at constructing fortress walls. Finally, after she'd gotten in the way one too many times, the bishop suggested that a better task for her might be running messages back and forth between the two defensive towers guarding the bridges on either side of the island.

She was just crossing through the center of the city on her way back north when someone fell into step next to her. She glanced over to find a teen boy, probably not much older than her, with closely cropped hair and an angular face. Immediately her guard went up—she recognized him as someone who'd been hovering around Riq, Dak, and her for much of the day, never far out of earshot.

"Lovely night," he said, and she grunted in response. That didn't keep him from trying to engage her in conversation. "I don't believe we've met before. Have you been in Paris long? Where are you from?"

It was a lot of questions for one stranger to ask

another, and Sera waved her hand in the air. "Here and there," she answered noncommittally as she picked up her pace.

The boy sped up as well. "I was born here, but my family's from Northumbria in Britain. Lindisfarne, actually. Have you heard of it?"

Sera cut a glare at him. She didn't really care where he was from and she didn't know why he kept talking to her.

Nevertheless, he pushed on. "My great-great-great-uncle was a monk there. At Lindisfarne Priory. He's who I'm named after, actually. Oh, I never did introduce myself properly. I'm Billfrith." He paused, clearly waiting for her to introduce herself, but she kept quiet—and kept moving. But the boy didn't take the hint.

"I guess not that many people have heard of Lindisfarne Priory these days, which is really a shame. During its time it was a great place of learning. The monks specialized in history, with a keen interest in Aristotle and his pupil Alexander."

This got Sera's attention, and she stopped abruptly. Her mind whirred over the riddle from the SQuare: "Upset the clue within: . . . Find a roofless inn." She began playing with the letters, "upsetting" their order until she found a new arrangement. Suddenly, "find a roofless inn" morphed into "son of Lindisfarne."

She sucked in a breath. "Wait, what was that last bit?"

Billfrith had to double back. "My ancestors were monks at Lindisfarne Priory, which was once the greatest library in the world. They'd collected more information about Aristotle than anyone else. The priory was destroyed in a raid by the Danes over a century ago, and my great-great-great-uncle was the only one who survived. He's passed down everything he knew. Everyone in my family is quite the, ah, *historian.*" He smiled. "Including me."

5

A Secret Breach

DAK KNEW Sera would be furious, but that didn't stop him from sneaking from the north tower and slipping into the darkness of the mainland. It had been ages since Sera had gone to deliver a message to the south tower, and Dak had no idea how much longer the darkness would last; they'd had to ditch their watches after their first time warp so they wouldn't look suspicious. He still hadn't gotten used to telling time by the movement of the stars or sun, and he wasn't willing to risk losing the chance to check out the Viking ships firsthand.

Besides, Sera had left the SQuare with him and he had it tucked into a satchel slung across his shoulder, so technically he was still trying to work out the code they'd found earlier. He just wasn't doing it at that exact moment.

Escaping Riq's notice was easy once the older boy began nodding off as the night stretched on. And since the tower was situated on the mainland, he didn't have to risk crossing the bridge and getting noticed. Really, all he needed to do was not appear suspicious. He'd learned a long time ago that if you looked like you belonged, people tended to ignore you. It worked just as well in the ninth century as it had in the twenty-first.

November in Paris turned out to be pretty cold once he was away from the light and warmth of the tower, and the clothes Riq had found weren't all that warm. Dak shivered as he felt his way across the deep trough ringing the tower. Behind him, in the middle of the river, shadows paced back and forth along the wall around Paris, soldiers keeping an eye on the Viking camps.

Dak scrambled upriver, a long black stretch of water lapping softly along muddy banks to his left. A thin sheet of frost crackled under his feet as he slipped his way through fields and between the few houses and churchyards that had been built across from the island.

Even from here he sensed the fear of the coming morning radiating from the city, and this caused him to pause. He remembered catching a glimpse into one of the houses in Paris as he'd walked by earlier in the evening. He'd seen a father pull a young boy onto his lap, brushing frightened tears from his son's eyes. At the memory, something tightened inside Dak, making it harder to breathe as he thought about his own father, now lost in time. Sera theorized that his parents were being drawn to the Breaks and that eventually they'd find one another again, but Dak wasn't so sure.

In one swift moment Dak felt the enormity of the task the Hystorians had given the three of them and how easily it could all go wrong. For his entire life, the two things he'd always been sure of were his parents' love for him and his knowledge of history.

Now his parents were missing and history was changing.

Dak looked back at the north tower and thought about turning around. Sera would be worried. But then he felt the inescapable tug of the Viking ships moored up the river. It would only take a minute or two for him to scurry down and take a look. With the Vikings themselves encamped farther inland, he would never have a better opportunity.

Firsthand knowledge of Viking artifacts was rare in his time, and the thought of returning home and being able to straighten the record was too tempting an opportunity to pass up.

Dak hoped Sera had nodded off like Riq, but just in case he sent a silent apology over his shoulder and made his way quickly to the ships. They towered over him. The boat they'd seen (and almost been crushed by) during their class trip to the Smithsonian paled in comparison to the real thing. Dak reached out and pressed a hand against one of the hulls. The wood was smooth, painted in bright reds and blues, and without any blemishes or knots. Holes dotted the sides where oars could be set for rowing, and the prow curved into the form of a sinister-looking dragon's head.

Dak had told himself he'd just take a quick look and leave, but that was impossible. It wasn't enough to glance at the hull; he had to climb inside and sit on the benches and wrap his hands around a set of oars. Above him sails wound tight around spars attached to a forest of masts and he imagined the color of them all unfurled: red, yellow, white, blue, green.

He was so lost in his daydream that he didn't hear the crunch of approaching feet across the frosty bank. All Dak knew was that one minute he was standing on the prow of a Viking ship imagining all kinds of seafaring adventures, and the next he was flat on his back.

Pinning him to the deck was the largest beast Dak had seen in his entire life. It had paws the size of cement blocks resting on either side of Dak's ribs. But all Dak could really focus on was the monster's head, its mouth a cavern of sharp teeth. The animal panted a hot breath against Dak's face that stank of something truly horrid. When it growled, the entire boat vibrated.

This wasn't exactly the way Dak had imagined his life ending, but there was little he could do to defend himself. Instead he tried a little diplomacy.

"Nice doggie," he cooed. "Who's a good boy?"

This only caused the beast to draw its tongue over its lips in anticipation.

"Sit?" Dak tried again. The dog tilted its head to the side, as one long string of thick drool slid from its mouth and came within millimeters of Dak's cheek.

What Dak heard next almost scared him more than the beast pinning him to the deck. It was a low booming that sounded more like thunder than a man's laughter. The largest human being Dak had seen in his entire life leaned into the boat, causing it to tip precariously.

When the man spoke, Dak's earpiece immediately switched languages to translate. As soon as he heard the words, Dak thought that perhaps it would have been better if he'd been left in ignorance.

"Well, Vígi," the giant said, surveying the situation. "It seems like you found your own dinner after all."

Sera couldn't stop pacing. "Where is he?" She'd asked the question a million times before and she knew that Riq didn't have an answer, but that didn't stop her from repeating herself. She couldn't *believe* Dak had just snuck out without telling anyone. They'd had an agreement: First they'd find the Hystorian, then he could look at one Viking ship. (And while technically she'd found the Hystorian, Dak hadn't known that, which meant he'd totally broken the rule.)

Already the sky was lightening, which meant that at any minute the Vikings would begin attacking the city. She couldn't bear the thought of Dak out there alone. She sat and put her head in her hands. "I'm going to kill him," she muttered, but her threat was halfhearted.

What would she do if she lost him for good?

She shivered and pushed the thought from her mind. Thankfully, she had something else to focus on. "Okay, Billfirth," she said, turning to the Hystorian.

"Billfrith," he corrected.

She frowned. "That's what I said."

"No," Riq corrected. "You said -*firth*, not -*frith*."

She took a deep breath before finally suggesting, "How about I just call you Bill?" He smiled back at her, which she took to be his consent.

"So," Sera continued. "Now that we've found you, you can tell us what we're supposed to be doing here, right?"

Bill looked uneasily between the two of them. "I can tell you historically what's led us to this point, but I can't tell you what the Break is or how it was, or will be, caused. That's something that can only be determined from the future—after it's happened."

Sera reached to tug on her hair, a habit to ease frustration, but then she remembered that it had mostly been cut off during their first time warp. Instead she sighed and placed her hands in her lap.

"Seems we've exchanged one useless history buff for another," Riq grumbled.

Sera shot him a pointed look. "Mari and Brint wouldn't have told us to find Hystorians if they didn't think we'd need the help."

"I'm not questioning whether we need the help," Riq countered. "I'm questioning whether this kid is going to be able to provide it."

Sera saw Bill frown at being called a kid, and her cheeks flushed a bit with embarrassment at how rude Riq was being.

"I *can* tell you that there's an SQ contingent within the Viking ranks," Bill said. "That's useful information."

"We already figured that out," Riq snapped.

Sera had had enough. "Hey, we all have the same goal here — how about we work together?"

Riq's only response was to frown and pace to a narrow opening in the tower wall. They were all feeling on edge. They'd already meddled with the path of history, and none of them knew what the effects of that would be. During the night the Parisians had been able to make the north tower taller by half, but it didn't seem possible that it would be enough to stave off the impending Viking attack.

She'd just turned back to Bill to ask him more about what he knew when Riq drew in a sharp breath. When he looked at them his face was grim. "Well, the good news is, I've found Dak. The bad news is, so have the Vikings."

Rollo the Walker

THE MASSIVE dog drew its tongue up the length of Dak's face as if giving him a taste. If Dak had thought the creature's breath was bad, its drool was even worse. He tried to hold his own breath against the stench of it. "Please don't eat me," he squeaked.

The giant leaning over the edge of the boat laughed. "Enough, Vígi," he commanded. "This one's too scrawny for a meal." The dog huffed before jumping off Dak and landing by its master's side.

Dak sat up, wiping at his cheek. "Ugh, what do you feed that thing? Molded cheese? And I don't mean the good kind, like a nice Roquefort."

The man looked at Dak meaningfully. "Sometimes. When we can't find Franks to satisfy her appetite."

The response caused Dak to swallow nervously. Did the Viking think Dak was an enemy scout? Best to play dumb, he decided. "Uh, no Parisians here, though. Maybe we can find one for her?" He stood and began making his way aft to climb down, keeping as far away from the Viking—and his dog—as possible.

Apparently, the Viking wasn't ready for Dak to leave, because he shoved the edge of the boat into the water, causing the deck to pitch and Dak to fall against one of the benches. "Yet you speak French as well as you speak my people's tongue." When Dak began to deny this the man added, "I heard you speaking to Vígi when I approached."

Dak remembered the excuse Riq used earlier and tried it out. "I like languages. I'm kind of a collector of them, you might say."

Apparently, this Viking wasn't as gullible as the others. He pursed his lips. "Like the bishop's translator, *hmm*? Any other language scholars in the area I should know about?"

Dak shook his head. The less he said, the better. For all he knew, the Viking standing in front of him could be SQ—maybe even a Time Warden, in which case Dak was totally hosed. He needed to get back to the tower or, better yet, inside the walls of the city itself.

"Well, it was good talking but I should probably go. . . ."

Dak had just thrown a leg over the side of the boat and was sliding toward the shore when the Viking caught him in midair. With one hand. Dak's struggles were fruitless—the man's hand was so huge it almost circled his entire waist.

"No need to scamper off," the man boomed. "You entertain me. I think I'll keep you longer; you look useful. And if it turns out you're not, you can be Vígi's new toy. I think she's taken a liking to you."

Hearing her name, Vígi pulled her lips back from her teeth. Dak couldn't tell if the dog was grinning or just showing Dak how close he'd come to being dinner (and how such a possibility still wasn't entirely out of the question).

Something sharp dug into Dak's hip and he realized that it was the edge of the SQuare. If the Vikings got ahold of that, he really would be in massive trouble. There was no way he could come up with an explanation for that sort of thing.

His mind spun frantically, trying to figure out what to do. The Viking released his grip to place Dak upon the ship's edge, and Dak took that moment to drop his satchel onto the deck of the ship, behind one of the large round shields set along the hull. It was hidden from plain view, but not particularly well.

With a deep sense of unease, Dak allowed himself to fall to the ground. When he found himself face-to-face with the Viking's belly button, he realized just how huge the guy was.

"Rollo the Walker," the man said, thumping a massive fist against his chest.

Dak scrunched his face up in confusion. "Walker?"

The Viking grinned hugely. "On account of there not being any horse large enough to carry a man as big as me. Who are you?"

"Dak," he answered. It seemed like Rollo expected more. "Uh, Dak the, er . . . Cheese Eater?"

That earned another bellowing laugh from the giant. "We'll see what we can scrounge up for you back at camp, then. There may be some headcheese left if you're lucky."

Dak's stomach growled at the mere mention of his favorite food. "I've never heard of that one," he said, his mouth already watering. "Is it goat cheese or cow?"

"Cow." Rollo began walking away from the river, toward the burning fire pits spread across the countryside.

Dak wasn't about to let him get far when there was cheese to discuss. "Are we talking something hard, like Parmesan, or softer, like a nice creamy Brie?"

Rollo glanced at him with an odd expression. "I'd probably describe it as 'squishy,' but then I like to leave the eyes and brain in. Otherwise you're just left with flesh, tongue, and maybe some heart, and where's the texture in that?"

"What? Why would you . . . ?" Dak couldn't even finish the thought—his stomach was too busy turning over. "Eyes? Brain? How could you ruin cheese like that?"

Rollo's smile was huge and showed a few too many teeth for Dak's comfort. "*Headcheese,* I said. It's like a meat jelly made from the head of a cow. I'll give you a taste when we get to camp."

Rollo gestured for Dak to get moving.

"Wait!" Alarmed, Dak glanced back at the north tower. Behind it a strip of hazy light began to creep up the horizon. It wouldn't be long before the battle started. "I was just thinking that I'd scout out around the Parisian defenses, maybe see if there are any weaknesses for you to exploit in the morning. You know what they say, a prepared Viking is a . . . er . . . prepared."

46

He tried to smile, but even Vígi whuffed in disdain.

Rollo leaned down until his face was right in front of Dak's. "Let me be blunt. You intrigue me, but that doesn't mean I trust you. I still haven't made up my mind if you're friend or foe, and I like to keep both close at hand. Either way, you're not getting out of my sight. Try, and I'll have to send my best warrior out after you." He set his hand on Vígi's head, indicating just who his best warrior was. "And she is not known for her mercy."

7

War Machines

SERA STARED out the window at where Dak cowered in the shadow of a massive Viking. Her heart pounded heavily in her chest, and her voice had an edge of panic. "We need to go out after him."

She'd already started for the tower stairs when Riq put his hand on her shoulder. "We have a job to do, Sera," he said. "If we go out there and get captured, how are we going to fix the Break?"

"He needs our help," she snapped at him, but Riq still didn't let her go. Sera closed her eyes, trying to find patience, but there was nothing left. She didn't understand how he could be hesitating. It was *Dak* out there beyond the fortress walls, and he clearly needed their help.

"I think there's a bigger problem you two are forgetting," Bill suggested.

Sera glared at him. "I *know* what we're supposed to be doing," she snapped. "But sometimes saving your best friend is more important than saving the world!"

"What about saving yourself?" he asked.

Sera frowned, not understanding. Bill pointed out the window. "I'd say we have about five, maybe ten minutes before the Vikings attack us with everything they've got. And what they've got is a whole lot more force than we have."

She didn't want to, but Sera peeked out the window facing the mainland. What she saw made her head spin. In the few moments she'd spent arguing, the Vikings had rolled massive wooden contraptions into view. She had no idea what they were, but she had a sinking suspicion that she'd find out soon enough.

Bill joined her by the window. "Ballistae," he said. "War machines they'll use to fling huge stones. And that's just their opening move."

"We have to do something," she whispered.

Riq and Bill exchanged glances. "There's only one thing we really can do," Bill offered.

Sera sighed, already fearing the answer. "And what's that?"

Riq held out a bow and a quiver of arrows as if she'd have any idea how to use them. "We have to fight."

In the distance Sera heard the first Viking war horn begin to blow. It was followed by another and another until the air was swollen with the sound of them. "But what if we fail? What if the Vikings take Paris after all?"

Once again Bill glanced at Riq, and Sera was pretty sure there was some sort of silent communication between them that she wasn't a part of. "Let's hope it doesn't come to that," he finally said as the first of the

Viking catapults let loose with a barrage of stones and arrows.

Rollo had shoved Dak into a tent, set Vígi at the entrance to guard him, and then traipsed off to the battlefield. Dak protested as much as he could—not only did he absolutely have to get back to Sera, but he also wasn't keen on the idea of completely missing the battle. That just wasn't fair!

At first Dak tried to sneak past Vígi, but even when she seemed in the deepest sleep (as indicated by ear-shattering snores), the moment Dak reached for the tent flap she'd leap to her feet and growl so loud he felt the air hum.

In the end, he came up with a foolproof plan. Vígi was just like every other dog he'd ever known: Give her a solid ten minutes of scratching behind the ears and she'd pledge her life to you. In fact, his plan to win her over worked too well—she tried to follow him out onto the battlefield several times until he finally had to find a length of rope and tie her to a support pole in the tent.

"Sorry, girl," he said, giving her a good rub under the chin when she looked up at him mournfully. "I don't want you getting hurt," he added. Her expression seemed to ask, "What about you?" which was a question Dak didn't want to think about.

He'd found a pair of pants and a slightly flared wool tunic and had exchanged his Frankish clothes so that he'd blend in easier with the Viking horde. It seemed to work, because as he walked through the camp no one paid him any mind. From there it was just a matter of following the sounds of battle.

Dak figured he had read more about war than anyone he knew. He'd memorized casualty lists and studied time lines of weapons development and learned battle strategy, and until this moment he'd have called himself an expert.

But real war was nothing like the accounts he'd read in books. First, there was the noise—it was so much louder than he'd ever expected. Men shouted commands, trebuchets launched piles of stones, and ballistae shot javelins into the air; horns blared and church bells rang. Then there were the smells: smoke from fires set against the walls around the city, blood from open wounds, the earthy stench of mud and sweat.

His fingers itched for his SQuare diary to record it all with. In his mind he imagined returning home, sharing his firsthand account, and becoming a famous historian. He'd be a world-renowned expert and when he opened his mouth to share random bits of history, people would listen without laughing or rolling their eyes.

Just as his daydream culminated with him walking across the stage to receive the Nobel Prize, he was interrupted by harsh reality.

"You, boy!" someone shouted angrily. Dak glanced over his shoulder, attempting to look innocent. He recognized the Viking who was approaching him. It was one of the men who'd accompanied Siegfried into the chapel the previous morning—the one named Gorm, with the bright red scar slashing from eyebrow to chin, who had seemed suspicious of Riq's ability to speak both Old Norse and French. "Don't you think you're a little out of time?" he asked Dak now.

The question sounded harmless enough, but Dak grasped its double meaning. Gorm knew Dak wasn't supposed to be there, that he was from another century.

Which meant that Dak was in big trouble if Gorm got his hands on him.

So Dak ran—right into the heart of the battlefield.

8

Under Attack

SERA WATCHED the first bombardment of stones in wonder. So many projectiles filled the air that it was almost impossible to see the sky. It wasn't until Bill shoved her away from the tower's window and crouched over her that she truly understood what was about to happen.

Or rather, what had just begun. The tower shuddered under the onslaught. Stones splintered walls. Arrows zinged through the open window, embedding in the wooden floor by her feet.

"We have to find someplace safe!" Riq shouted, and they crawled toward the stairs. A sea of Franks pushed against them, racing toward the top of the tower to take up defensive positions. The men wore battle dress: thickly padded tunics and metal helmets. Some carried swords and shields, and others had bows and arrows. Just looking at them made Sera feel more vulnerable in her simple woolen tunic.

"This way," Bill urged, taking her elbow and pulling her into a narrow, dark corridor. She'd only taken a few steps when she heard Riq grunt behind her. She turned to find him being pulled in the opposite direction by a large Frankish soldier.

"Only two hundred men on this side of the river to defend the tower," the soldier said, shoving a wicked-looking sword into Riq's hands. His wrist bent awkwardly under the weight of it. "We need all the manpower we can get." He began dragging Riq up the stairs.

"Wait!" Sera called out. She swallowed and tried to keep her voice from shaking. "I'll help, too," she offered. She'd already been separated from Dak; she couldn't lose Riq as well. Behind her, Bill hissed for her to be quiet.

The soldier squinted at her as if seriously considering her offer and then scoffed. "You should be back across the river with the other children. What you're still doing here I don't know, but you're well and trapped now." He nudged Riq toward the staircase where he was swallowed up by the rush of men. "You want to help?" the man asked. "Stay out of our way." And then he, too, was gone.

Sera tried to run after them but Bill kept his hand tight around her arm. "He's right, Sera," he said, but she didn't want to hear it. She felt like she was losing complete control of everything. Dak's role was to use his historical knowledge to figure out the Breaks and how to fix them. Riq's job was to make sure they could always communicate with those around them. That left Sera, whose only contribution was to make sure the Infinity Ring warped them to the right place and time.

And even that wasn't so complicated that Dak or Riq couldn't figure it out if they needed to.

Which meant that Sera's real responsibility was keeping the three of them together. They'd been in 885 for less than twenty-four hours and she'd already failed. Miserably.

As if sensing how upset Sera was, Bill gently squeezed her arm. "He'll be okay," he said. "They both will."

Sera shook her head. "How can you know? Everything about history has already changed, thanks to us, and we don't know if it's for the better or worse."

He took her hand in his, which felt a little awkward at first until they sorted their fingers out. "From my point of view, I can definitely say it's changed for the better," he said softly, causing Sera to blush.

She really wasn't sure how to respond to that. Ever since they'd left home, she'd been so focused on fixing the Breaks that it never occurred to her to think about how their meddling with history affected those they met along the way. She thought about the first Hystorian they'd met, Gloria the butcher, and how her eyes had grown wide when they told her about airplanes and men on the moon. Did she then spend the rest of her life dreaming about such things, or did she go about her ordinary duties as if she'd never met three kids from the future?

Just then, there was a tremendous crashing sound. A few stones fell from the ceiling and shattered at her feet. A long crack snaked up the wall, letting in a slice of sunlight and the sound of men shouting and swords clashing. Another jolt jarred the tower, and Sera and Bill stumbled as they tried to catch their footing.

"It isn't safe here," Bill shouted at her over the din of battle. "Follow me." And then he was leading her through the dim corridor, his hand still holding hers tightly.

They passed a few narrow slits in the walls that Bill explained were arrow loops, meant to allow men inside to fire arrows on anyone attacking. As they passed by each one, Sera snuck glances outside, trying to catch glimpses of the battle. Hundreds of ships lined the river, each one stuffed with men wearing chain mail and helmets, waving swords or shooting at the tower with bows and arrows. All of them moved toward the bridge, disgorging their cargo of soldiers on the nearby shore. Here they joined others digging at the foundation of the tower with pickaxes and shovels, trying to tunnel under the thick wall.

Along the northern bank more Vikings prepped trebuchets and catapults, lobbing stones and flaming pots of oil over the walls of the fortified city. The sky was thick with projectiles, the air dingy with smoke and loud with shouting and screaming. Church bells rang and Viking horns blew as if the two sides could war with sound alone.

Bill drew her through a tight passage into a tiny circular room with a high domed ceiling. "It's an old turret," he said. "They changed the design of the tower after this room was built, and most people forget about it. We should be safe here for a while. At least until the bridge clears enough for us to sneak back to the city."

Narrow gaps were spread along the wall at knee height and Sera pressed her face against one. "Murder holes," Bill explained. He pointed out how the sides of the holes flared out at steep angles, narrowing the view. "Men can kneel here and shoot crossbows, picking off soldiers outside, but it's almost impossible to get an arrow back in."

He leaned against one of the walls and slid until he was sitting. His legs took up a good portion of the floor space, so that Sera had to sit with her knees tucked against her chest. She could still feel the floor trembling beneath her as stones struck the tower. Even though it meant watching the ravaging forces attacking them, she couldn't help but look outside, trying to catch a glimpse of Dak.

She hoped he was smart enough to keep far, far away from the battlefront. But she also knew him well enough to be pretty sure he'd never stay away from the center of action. "Please don't be stupid," she murmured to herself.

As if on cue, her eye caught on a small figure darting through the throng of Vikings. Sera had been in enough PE classes with Dak to recognize his awkward gait as he ducked behind a pile of discarded bloody shields.

"Dak!" she cried out, banging her hand against the wall. But all she could do was watch, and hope none of the flying debris—from either side—would hit her friend.

This wasn't like dodgeball (a game that Dak never excelled at)—these flying balls could kill!

A single shield detached itself from the pile and

started moving haltingly across the battlefield. The wooden circle was huge, at least as tall as Dak, and he teetered under the weight of it. A band of Vikings streamed around him, racing toward the tower with bloodcurdling shouts and roars, but one of them must have knocked into Dak because he tripped and went sprawling.

Just as he started to push himself up, a massive bolt shot from the tower and tore through the air. It barely grazed Dak's head before skewering seven Vikings who'd been running along behind him.

From somewhere above she heard men cheering as one of them shouted, "Tell the kitchens we have a human kabob for them to cook!"

Sera cried out as the men staggered and then fell. Dak's face went white with shock and he crouched, seemingly frozen, completely out in the open where anyone could take aim at him.

She heard someone screaming and realized belatedly that it was her, calling Dak's name and telling him to move.

9

Bearing the Standard

DAK COULDN'T move. The bolt had come so close to his head he could swear it had created a new part in his hair. He heard the sickening sound of the sharp metal tip striking the Vikings who'd been running behind him and then the grunt as they collapsed. Dark red blood seeped from their chests, turning the ground around them to a scarlet mud.

The reality of where he was and what he was doing struck him like a battering ram against a fortress gate. He was unarmed and unarmored in the middle of a chaotic battlefield. On the positive side, he'd put some distance between himself and Gorm. But getting killed now wouldn't be helping anyone, least of all himself.

For the briefest moment the violence around him paused, and he thought he heard someone scream his name. He stared up at the tower only a hundred yards away, trying to seek out a familiar face. It was useless, and he knew it. Riq and Sera would be safe inside the island fortress by now—far, far away from the danger of battle.

But then he thought he heard that same voice shout for him to move. He didn't even question where the command came from. Instead, he just obeyed, tucking into a ball and rolling sharply to his left.

An arrow whizzed through the air with a high-pitched whine, striking the shield underneath Dak with a solid *thwunk*. Two inches to the left and it would have speared his shoulder.

That's all it took to get Dak to his feet and sprinting back toward the Viking camp—facing Gorm seemed like the better option at the moment. As he ran he cut from right to left to make himself a more difficult target. He'd just crested a low hill when he saw a line of Vikings—hundreds of them—racing for the battlefield, their shields held over their heads to protect themselves from the rain of stones and arrows.

It was pretty clear pretty fast that Dak would be trampled to death if he kept going. He had no option but to pivot on his heel and run along with them, letting himself get caught up in their roaring energy. Tucked among the massive bodies and huge round shields, Dak felt nearly safe.

It was almost as if he were one of them.

As they approached the tower the sound of stones hitting shields became as deafening as the screaming around him. A reed-thin boy holding a tall pole with a pennant streaming from the top grinned at Dak as they ran alongside each other. Dak had just started to smile back when the boy's eyes went wide and his teeth turned a pinkish red. When he fell to his knees, Dak saw a thick spear protruding from between his shoulder blades.

Horrified, Dak took a step forward—his instinct was to offer help even though he knew there was nothing he could do. The boy said nothing, just held out the pole, shoving it into Dak's hands before collapsing. Dak stood there, his hands gripping the pole, no idea what to do next.

One of the other Vikings must have seen the look of terror and confusion on Dak's face, because he slapped his back in what was probably meant to be a reassuring gesture but ended up sending a jolt of pain through him.

"You're the standard-bearer now, boy." He gestured up at the flag. "That's Siegfried's seal there. Upon your life, you cannot let it fall. Best watch yourself—holding it makes you a target. The Franks would do anything to get that flag as proof of victory."

And then the man was off, and Dak was left in the middle of battle staring up at the scrap of cloth hanging limply from the top of the pole. A sluggish bit of breeze found its way to him, lifting the flag so that he could see the banner clearly. If his heart wasn't already frozen in fear, it would have sprouted icicles.

He recognized the symbol Siegfried used for his standard. He'd seen it before on the lapels of Tilda the Lady in Red, etched into the belt buckles of the Amancio brothers, and scraped into a wall in 1792 Paris. It was the symbol of the SQ, and it was apparently now Dak's responsibility to protect it.

∞

"What in the name of mincemeat is Dak thinking?" Sera groaned. She and Bill knelt side by side, staring out the murder hole to where Dak stood, holding a flag that lifted in the meager breeze. "He's just made himself a target!"

Beside her, Bill tensed and cursed under his breath, using a word the device in her ear refused to translate.

"What is it?" she asked, dread already pooling in her stomach.

"I recognize the emblem on that standard," he said. "It's the symbol of the men who attacked Lindisfarne."

Sera frowned. "The symbol of the SQ. That's why we're here—Siegfried is SQ, and we have to stop him from amassing power."

Bill pressed his face against the hole again and spoke as she did the same. "It's not just that one banner I'm worried about. It's all the others."

Sera let her eyes roam across the battlefield. Now that she was looking for something other than Dak, she realized that half the men bore some form of the SQ symbol. It was carved into helmets, painted on the hulls of ships, even woven into the cloaks thrown over Viking shoulders.

"They're everywhere," she said in shock.

Bill turned until he was facing her and she could feel the warm puffs of his breath against her cheek. "Is there any way they could know that you're here?"

She shook her head. "No, not unless . . ." She caught herself just as she was about to mention Dak. She knew he wouldn't have said anything to give the three of them away. Then she remembered the Viking who'd accompanied Siegfried to the cathedral — the one with the scar across his face.

"There was one of Siegfried's men that seemed like he might have been suspicious. Why?"

Bill leaned back against the wall, his hands worrying along the edge of his dagger. "You represent a threat to the power it's taken the SQ eleven centuries to amass. If they even suspect there's someone from the future behind these walls, they'll stop at nothing to get to you."

Sera looked back at the battlefield. There were soldiers for as far as she could see. Individually they were like drops of water that combined to create a massive ocean. "How can we hope to fight so many?"

Bill hesitated before answering, which, Sera was coming to realize, was never a good sign.

"I think you have to face the possibility that Paris might fall," he said at last. "And if that happens, you have no choice but to warp out of here and keep the Infinity Ring from falling into SQ control."

10

Taking a Dive

DAK SPENT most of the next few hours trying to avoid getting killed, which wasn't as easy as it sounded. Even though the Franks were wildly outnumbered, they had the benefit of thick walls between them and the Vikings. Plus, they were fighting to defend their homes, which made them especially formidable.

To make his task of staying alive (and in one piece) even more difficult, Dak wore no armor and carried no weapons. He just had the stupid flag, which meant he couldn't sneak away either. Every time he tried to hand it off to someone else he was met with hearty slaps on the back and congratulations for making it as long as he had. Apparently, standard-bearer was a very short-term gig with a high mortality rate.

The only benefit to his position was that he had plenty of time to race around the fortifications, searching for a way inside. He knew that trying to use force would be useless — if thirty thousand Vikings couldn't break down the wall, what hope did an eleven-year-old boy have?

His only chance would be to use his brain, which was overflowing with tales of fortresses being taken in various ways. His favorite had always been the story of Château Gaillard, a supposedly impenetrable medieval castle. Among its many features was an extra bathroom built in the chapel. Following the orders of King John of England, a little room had been constructed so that it hung off the side of the building, with a hole in the floor. It's what passed for luxury in those days.

When the French king Phillip II attacked Château Gaillard, the people inside felt pretty secure about being able to wait out the siege. But then came a soldier named Ralph the Snubnose who noticed a stain under a hole off to the side of one of the walls, and, using the nose for which he was named, figured out what the hole was used for.

That unlucky soldier had to climb his way up the toilet chute and through the hole to get into the castle (ew!). It worked—the guy surprised everyone inside and opened the gate to let his army in.

If that's what it took for Dak to find a way back to Sera and Riq, he was willing to try it—which is how he found himself staring up at the top of the tower when the men inside rolled a massive stone grinding wheel until it tottered just on the edge. One tiny tap and the thing would come crashing down.

Dak stood next to a group of Vikings wielding pickaxes against the base of the wall. They were so focused on their task that they had no idea of the danger looming above. Dak didn't even pause to think about the fact that some of these Vikings were with the SQ . . . which technically made them the bad guys.

"Move!" he shouted. He swung his pole around to shove two of the men back and then dove at a third, tackling him to the ground and rolling.

The stone wheel seemed to fall in slow motion, like a clip from an action movie. Dak could have sworn he felt the compression of air around him as a circular shadow grew larger until it seemed to swallow him.

He was pretty sure he was about to be squashed like a bug.

At the last minute he tucked his knees to his chin, just as the wheel slammed into the ground, barely missing his toes. The impact caused his teeth to jar and his whole body to lift into the air.

Men cried out in anguish. One of them had both of his legs pinned, and Dak thought he might have seen a hand sticking out from underneath — the hand of someone who'd been crushed and killed.

Around him Vikings leapt into action, striving to pull the injured men free as smaller stones and arrows fell around them. Dak tried to control his breathing, tried not to vomit all over himself as he dug into the mud to help. He felt his chin wobble and his throat burn with the promise of tears.

With great effort he swallowed them back. He glanced up at the tower, where Frankish soldiers leaned out over the edge, taunting the injured and dead below.

Suddenly, the lines that seemed so clear when they'd

warped here became fuzzy. He knew that many of the Vikings must be SQ and therefore his enemy. At the same time, he'd spent the afternoon with these men, listening to their shouts as they worked together and fought together, sometimes even trading jokes. They had protected him with their shields and accepted him as their bannerman.

They couldn't all be evil, could they? And even if they were . . . did they deserve to die like this?

Dak was still trying to sort it all out when he saw what looked like a curl of smoke rising up from the top of the tower. Riq appeared then, leaning over and shouting something down at Dak, but there was too much noise for him to catch what the older boy was saying. What on earth was he doing up there to begin with?

Riq began to wave his arms frantically, but it wasn't until Dak saw the lip of a steaming cauldron that he understood what he was trying to say. Riq was warning Dak, telling him to get out of the way. Already drops of the burning viscous liquid were falling like rain, hitting the ground around him with popping and hissing sounds.

Dak looked at the Viking soldiers grouped around the injured men, their shields held over their heads to keep their fallen comrades safe. They had no idea what was coming. He wanted to save them — but it was already too late.

Riq's expression was bleak when he stumbled upon Sera and Bill. As soon as she laid eyes on him, Sera's stomach tightened into frightened knots. "What's wrong?"

Riq said only one word, his voice almost a whisper. "Dak."

She leapt to her feet, ignoring the way her hands were beginning to tremble.

He's okay, she thought. He just had to be. But the longer Riq avoided her eyes the more she began to fear the rest.

Bill stood and moved next to her, his arm just barely brushing her shoulder. His hand slipped into hers and she squeezed, not realizing until that moment what it meant to have someone by her side for whatever Riq was about to say next.

"What happened?" she whispered.

Riq shook his head. "It was chaos." He drew in a deep breath as if to steel himself to say the words aloud. "Dak was with a band of Vikings trying to dig under the tower. They . . ." He swallowed a few times. "The Franks dropped cauldrons of hot pitch and wax down on top of them."

Sera felt like the floor was dropping away from her. The sensation was similar to the aftereffect of a Remnant: nausea, dizziness, and a confusion about time and space.

Riq wiped a hand across his face. "I didn't realize it was happening until it was too late, or I would have stopped it."

"Did you see his . . ." No matter how hard Sera struggled, she couldn't bring herself to say the word *body*.

But it was clear Riq knew what she was asking. "Some of them jumped into the river. . . ."

A ribbon of hope began to thread its way through Sera. "So he could have escaped? He could still be alive."

Riq hesitated before answering, and the pause buoyed her sense of optimism for a moment before it all came crashing down.

"Sera, the ones who dove into the Seine were on fire—that's why they were so desperate for water." His voice broke as he added, "I saw Dak's body floating down the river. He was facedown, and he wasn't moving."

11

The Dead Man's Float

DAK FOUGHT his way to the surface of the river, his lungs burning. He'd only recently been tossed overboard from the *Santa María*, and he hadn't survived that to end up drowning now.

Finally, his head broke free and he felt fresh air on his cheeks. His first breath was a choking wheeze that sputtered into coughing. Around him the battle still raged, though the tenor of it had changed. Small flames peppered the ground at the base of the tower, but most of the Vikings who had just been fighting there were gone.

Dak couldn't bear looking at any of the nearby bodies. It was too much — too real that the men he'd been working alongside were now dead. His stomach twisted, and he gagged on a mouthful of vile river water.

It didn't take Dak long to realize he was a target while treading water in the middle of the river, but his options were severely limited. The wall prevented him from climbing to land on the island side. And men who staggered to shore on the mainland were quickly brought down by arrows and bolts. Those seemed to be the lucky ones—other Vikings fought to pull off their heavy armor even as it dragged them down into the depths of the water.

Throughout all of this the Franks taunted their enemy, shouting: "Right badly burned, aren't you! Go jump in the river to save your flowing manes!"

Dak was really beginning to hate those guys, and not just because they were trying to kill him. Which gave him an idea: If they wanted him dead, so be it.

He slumped in the water, letting his body go limp. His back bobbed along the surface as his legs dragged below. The current tugged at him, pulling him away from the tower and the bridge to safety.

Every now and again he lifted his head, just barely, to take in a lungful of air. When they'd taught him the dead man's float at the pool for PE, he'd thought it was useless (even though it was the only thing he was really good at in that class) and he hadn't resisted letting his teacher know how he felt.

As Dak floated to safety he made a mental note to find Mr. Foltz and thank him when he got back to his own time.

Something cold nudged Dak's hand. He'd been washed ashore ages ago and even though he was drenched with foul river water and freezing, he wasn't taking any chances. That's why he'd spent the last several hours playing dead and didn't plan on moving until dark. But curiousity got the best of him now. He cracked open an eye and came face-to-face with rows of sharp, gleaming teeth.

Dak had never been a really great actor, and he completely broke character now — no one was going to believe he was dead once he yelped and started to scrabble backward. He didn't get far before a very wet and very smelly tongue lapped his face from chin to hair.

He recognized the stench immediately. "Ew, Vígi," he grumbled as he wiped the drool from his cheeks. "We need to find you a toothbrush!"

In response the dog nudged him, her nose prodding at his hand until he relented and tangled his fingers in her ears. She sat with a thud and then slipped to the ground, rolling against him with her four paws in the air.

"I think she likes you," a voice barreled. "Though you'd be the first."

Dak raised his eyes to find Rollo towering above him. He carried a huge sword in his meaty fist, and Dak couldn't stop staring at it. The double-edged blade was probably almost as long as he was tall.

It was just his luck that he'd avoided being crushed, pierced, burned, and drowned only to die under a giant's sword just when he thought things were beginning to look up.

At least the blade appeared sharp so his death would be quick.

Rollo must have sensed the direction of Dak's thoughts because he glanced at his sword and started to laugh, a sound like thunder. "Sorry," he said, slipping the weapon into a leather scabbard hanging on his left hip. "I didn't mean to let *Kettlingr* scare you."

Except that when the device in Dak's ear translated *Kettlingr*, Dak couldn't hold back the snort of laughter. "Wait, you named your sword *Kitten*? As in 'meow'?"

Rollo scowled, which was a pretty terrifying sight that caused Dak to choke on his giggles. "If you've ever been on the wrong end of a ticked-off kitten, you know how ferocious they can be."

Dak fell into a spasm of coughing to hide his amusement, which only caused Rollo to slam his palm against Dak's back as if to help, truly knocking the wind out of him. While Dak struggled for air, the Viking hauled him to his feet.

"Let's head back to camp," he said, gesturing down the river in the direction of light on the horizon. "Fighting's over for the day and it's time for dinner. I'd already be eating if it weren't for Vígi and her whining. She wouldn't shut up until I agreed to let her look for you."

The dog in question sat next to Dak, mouth open in a grin as she panted happily away. He tweaked her ears and she leaned against him, almost knocking him over.

"I really need to, er . . ." He glanced up at the side of a nearby ship, desperate for an excuse. He knew that so long as anyone was watching him, there was no way for him to recover the SQuare and sneak back into the fortified city. "I should really check to make sure none of the shields have splinters. You know how that can be out on the battlefield. Nothing worse, really."

This elicited a hearty laugh. "Nonsense," Rollo boomed. "You've distinguished yourself today, held the standard high, and saved many lives. Men back at camp want to honor you and share food." He then frowned. "Trust me when I say these are not men you want to keep waiting."

Dak remembered how ferocious the soldiers had been on the battlefield, and imagining them turning their ire on him was enough to propel him along the riverbank with Rollo.

Besides, the thought of real, actual Viking warriors wanting to thank Dak for his bravery? That was an experience he didn't want to miss!

1 2

Learning a Secret

SERA TRIED to avoid looking at the faces of those she passed as she walked with Riq over the bridge and back to the fortified city. The night was dark, which helped, but she still couldn't help noticing the hollowness of everyone's eyes, the slump of their shoulders. Despite all the damage they had done, it was barely a dent in the Viking force. A batch of men was repairing the tower and trying to build onto it, but how long could the city really stand against such an onslaught?

As depressing as these thoughts were, it was better than thinking about Dak. Sera knew that Riq was convinced something terrible had happened to her best friend — that he might even be dead — but she refused to believe that. If something truly awful had happened to him, she'd have felt it.

It didn't make scientific sense and she knew it. Sera was usually the first one to dismiss what she called "mumbo jumbo psychic rubbish." Once, in third grade, a girl in class had argued that certain lines on a person's palm revealed how long that person would live, how successful they would be, and even if they would get married. Sera had been the one to explain how such ideas had no scientific basis. Her entire life had been ruled by facts and data rather than emotion.

But now she was relying purely on emotion—on her belief that Dak was still alive somewhere out in the Viking camp—and it frightened her.

"Bill told me he suggested we leave Dak and warp away," Riq said, interrupting her thoughts and breaking the silence. Bill had given them some sort of excuse about finding food and shelter, but really Sera knew he was leaving the two of them alone to figure out what to do next.

"Dak has the SQuare," Sera reminded Riq. "Without that we have no idea what the next Break is."

Riq stopped and put a hand on her arm. "But if we knew where to go next, would you warp away?"

She opened her mouth, but no answer came out.

"What if it were me out there instead?" he asked.

That answer came to her immediately: She'd probably leave him behind. Though she didn't voice it out loud her cheeks colored with embarrassment, which gave Riq his answer.

He grunted and looked away. "I know what the right answer is," he finally said. "Fixing the Breaks is more important than any one of us. And if I'm ever the one out there I hope you make the decision to leave me. It's not like I have much of anything to go back to." He crossed his arms over his chest.

This surprised Sera. "You have your parents. That's more than I have."

He lifted a shoulder. "Ever wonder how I can speak so many languages? Sure, I'm a prodigy." He flashed the cocky smile she was used to, but it disappeared quickly. "But I also have a lot of time on my own. Both my parents are Hystorians . . . that kind of thing takes over your life if you haven't noticed."

She frowned. "It doesn't have to."

In response Riq laughed. "Says the girl more than a millennium away from home."

Just when Sera thought she was getting to see a new side of Riq, one that wasn't cocky and bristly, he had to go and mess it up. Sera was tired of it. "Why do you always have to be such a pill?" she asked.

Riq seemed genuinely surprised by the question, which spurred her on.

"You're always arguing—bickering, more like it. Why can't you just get along with people?"

He opened his mouth to answer and then closed it before turning away. Sera watched how his shoulders tensed. "You experience Remnants, right?" he asked.

Sera was caught off guard. He knew the answer already, but it still seemed so personal. She usually only talked about the subject with Dak, even though he didn't really understand what it was like.

Sera nodded. The events of the past several days caught up to her all at once, and she allowed herself to slide down a wooden fence until she was sitting on hard-packed dirt. She pulled her knees to her chest and wrapped her arms around her legs.

"They used to be rare," she explained. "Sometimes I'd go to this old barn that stood on the edge of my uncle's property, and I'd just *know* that at any minute the door would be flung open and two people would come strolling out toward me. It felt like they —" She cut herself off, feeling embarrassed. She pressed her finger against the dirt, dragging it in the endless loops of the infinity sign.

Riq sat next to her, close enough that she could feel a bit of warmth from him. "They were what?" he prodded.

She shifted and shrugged, feeling uncomfortable sharing something so personal. "It just felt like I should know them," she said softly. "That they loved me more than anything else in the world."

There, she'd said it. The one secret that she'd never even shared with Dak. He had two parents who adored him and supported him, whereas she'd never known her parents. It was an absence her life always tilted around.

Riq didn't tell her she was stupid; he simply accepted everything she said as if he understood. "Your Remnants . . . they've been getting worse, haven't they?" he asked.

Sera sighed. "It started when we were on the *Santa María* and I caught a glimpse of myself in a mirror. And now I get Remnants sometimes when I just say something. Usually when I'm bossing Dak around." She tried to laugh a bit to ease the seriousness of their discussion.

Riq smiled, but it was halfhearted. He seemed distracted.

She decided to ask him the question that had been on her mind for days. "When we were on the *Santa María*, you mentioned that if we fixed the Breaks we wouldn't have to deal with Remnants anymore. You said that we were saving the world, but we were also saving ourselves." Sera took a deep breath. "So do you have them, too? Remnants?"

He nodded slowly, and she waited for him to say more. "Is it okay if . . ." He cleared his throat and shifted as if uncomfortable. "If I don't talk about it?"

Sera tried not to feel hurt and disappointed but it must have showed in her expression, because he leaned toward her until his shoulder bumped hers and added, "Yet. I'm just not ready to talk about it yet."

She bumped him back. If Riq wasn't ready yet, then she'd wait.

"But here's the thing that really scares me," he said. "Mine have been getting worse. Much, much worse. I can't go more than a few hours without experiencing one. I'm worried that something we're doing here is causing it to happen. That we've made a huge mistake." He turned, finally looking her in the eye. "What if we've made the effects of the Break worse rather than better?"

13

A Sinking Feeling

DAK WASN'T sure how much more he could take. He'd planned to start the day extra early by slipping away from camp while it was still dark, grabbing the SQuare, and finding a way back to Sera and Riq.

Things hadn't worked out that way. Apparently what Dak considered "extra early," the Vikings considered past time to get the day started. He was roused by the clamber of chain mail and armor, and the general hustle and bustle of men preparing for battle.

He tried to sneak away but only succeeded in joining with a band of soldiers headed toward the Seine. At first he had his hopes up that they'd use the boats to attack the bridge and tower and it would be easy for him to recover the SQuare.

But of course Dak was never that lucky. Instead he found himself stuck nearly all day with the job of gathering debris from the battlefield: broken siege engines, trampled plants, even the bodies of executed prisoners—anything and everything he could carry. All because someone had come up with the brilliant idea of filling in the shallows of the river so that the Vikings' infantry could get around the tower.

It was the most horrific job Dak could ever imagine — much, much worse than scrubbing the deck of the *Santa María* or sneaking around in the Parisian sewers during the French Revolution — and he was miserable. Time and time again, he looked for an opportunity to sneak away, but nothing ever presented itself.

Until he overheard a few men discussing their next brilliant plan: lighting a few ships on fire and guiding them down the river toward the bridge. And one of the ships they planned to use was the very one on which he'd hidden the SQuare.

Dak's heart sped up. The SQuare was their only lifeline to their own time period. If they lost the SQuare, they might as well give up on fixing any other Breaks.

They might as well give up on looking for his parents.

"I'll help," Dak volunteered, almost tripping over his own feet as he raced to catch up with the group of soldiers making their way to the ships. He waited for them to brush him off, but then he realized that two of them were men he'd saved the day before. They didn't turn him away but instead welcomed him with hearty slaps on his back.

Dak was surprised by how good it felt to be accepted into something so easily. He'd always been more of an outcast at school, made fun of for his habit of spouting random bits of history. That's one reason he and Sera were such good friends—being outcasts gave them something in common.

He'd have never guessed that he'd ever feel at home with a band of Viking warriors. As they made their way to the ships, gathering dried grasses and sticks, Dak watched his companions. Many of them weren't much older than Riq, but they had a look in their eyes that said they'd lived very different lives.

For them, there was no such thing as school or hanging out at museums or going to lectures given by world-renowned physicists. But the Vikings' lives also weren't only about war, as Dak had once thought. Most of these men were simply looking for a place to settle—land to work and women to marry. But because most of the Viking history was oral rather than written, so much information about them was lost over time. What written details did survive tended to be recorded by those who lost battles against the North Men, which made it easy to see why the portrayals were mostly negative. Sure, some of the Vikings were bloodthirsty, only interested in pillaging and killing, but that wasn't the majority.

Dak marveled at how he'd almost describe some of these men as friends. Which was why it was that much more difficult to share their food and camp, and yet also try to figure out ways to thwart their efforts at getting into the city.

The longer the Vikings were kept at bay, the better

chance the Hystorians had of keeping Siegfried from amassing power, and of fixing the Break. Which meant Dak had to sabotage the very people who'd accepted him as one of their own.

They split into several groups and spread out among the chosen ships to stuff them with the dried debris and prep them to be set on fire. Dak made sure he was assigned to the boat where he'd hidden the SQuare.

His heart pounded hard. What if someone else had found it first? What if it had somehow slipped free and was now on the bottom of the river, broken beyond repair? He climbed aboard and checked the shield he thought he'd hidden it behind.

It wasn't there.

Had it been moved? Did he just have the wrong spot? As Dak started to search the boat, someone tossed a flaming torch into the aft hull. The fire sparked instantly, eating along the deck and across benches. Overhead the sail roared, its fabric catching quickly.

Dak was running out of time fast. Heat buffeted him and sweat broke out across his forehead and neck. Twice he shied away from the crackle of the hungry fire, but he couldn't give up on finding the SQuare.

The boat started to make its way down the river away from the group of Vikings and toward the bridge. Dak was stuck on board, still frantically searching behind every shield. There were twenty-five along each side and so far he'd only checked out half of them.

From the shore, men shouted for him to jump, but

he couldn't give up. If the SQuare was destroyed, it wouldn't matter that Dak survived the fire—they'd never be able to fix the Great Breaks and avoid the Cataclysm.

Wind whipped around him, feeding the flames and sending smoke spiraling into the sky. The flaming ships were drawing dangerously close to the bridge. If the Vikings succeeded in catching the bridge on fire, it would collapse and they'd have free reign up the Seine to the cities and villages beyond.

That bridge wasn't just protecting Paris, but also the rest of France—and the future of Europe. It was the only thing keeping Siegfried and the rest of the SQ from amassing even more power.

Suddenly, Dak's priorities were split. He had to find the SQuare, but he also had to make sure the flaming boat didn't make it to the bridge. Which was more important?

With a sinking stomach, he abandoned the search for the SQuare and pulled out an axe he'd found among the battlefield debris. He began swinging it at a seam between two boards of the hull, trying to make an opening. The wood was thick and solid, and Dak despaired of making any headway, but heat from the fire must have already weakened it because a crack began to form.

Billowing smoke choked the air around him, making his eyes water and lungs burn. The fire burned fiercely, consuming everything as it made its way toward the bow where Dak hacked furiously at the hull.

The wood groaned in protest and then a spurt of water sprayed up through a small hole in the bottom of the boat. It only took three more whacks with the axe for a healthy amount of water to begin filling the boat, slowing its progress toward the bridge.

Dak was almost out of time. The fire had already eaten its way past the mast, destroying more than half of the shields along the way. As fast as possible Dak checked the rest of the ship for the SQuare. Water dragged at his feet, climbing up his calves.

He found the SQuare in the very last place left to be checked. The bag holding it was already drenched, and he pulled the SQuare free and slipped it into the waistband of his pants under his tunic.

With a whoop of success he leapt from the ship, land-ing knee-deep in the shallows of the river. As he fought his way against the current toward shore he watched as the ship took on more water and began listing to its side before capsizing and sinking just as its bow struck a grouping of rocks used to support the bridge.

The other boats fared no better, crashing against the sunken boat just shy of the bridge. It was a beautiful sight to Dak, and he felt a surge of pride at having accom-plished both tasks. He'd rescued the SQuare *and* kept the Vikings from scoring a hit against Paris. All in all, Dak was pretty much a hero as far as he was concerned.

Before he could gloat too much, Dak was forcibly spun around. Gorm, the scarred Viking, grabbed him by the tunic, almost lifting him from the ground. "You think you're clever, don't you?" His face was so close that spit flew from his mouth with every word, peppering Dak's cheeks.

"I . . ." He scrambled for some sort of excuse and came up empty. "I don't know what you're talking about."

The Viking wrenched the axe from Dak's grip and tossed it into the river. Dak started to protest but thought better of it.

Dak was caught. He struggled to get free of the man's grasp but it was useless. Without a weapon he had no hope against someone so much stronger and larger.

The Viking grinned in an unpleasant way, the scar across his face causing his features to twist. "I know someone who will be *very* interested in speaking with you."

14

A Call from the Future

IT STARTED raining when the sun set, and Sera was drenched. Her teeth chattered as she huddled under the shelter of an old empty barn.

"At least the weather put an end to most of the fighting," Bill suggested, trying to find something to be cheerful about. Sera only grunted in return. She couldn't stop thinking of her warm bed in her warm house in a time when such a thing as gas heat existed.

"I'd kill for a hot shower right now," she grumbled.

"A Jacuzzi would be even better," Riq agreed.

Bill looked between them, confused. "What's a shower?"

Sera glanced his way, her arms wrapped tightly around her chest to keep as much warmth pressed to her body as possible. It had hardly occurred to her before meeting the Hystorians that there would be a period in time when something as basic as a shower didn't exist.

"It's like a bath, but the hot water falls from a shower-head—from a contraption in the wall or ceiling, like a waterfall," she explained.

Bill still looked confused. "That sounds like a lot of work for your servants to heat that much water. How many buckets does it take?"

Sera opened her mouth and then closed it, looking to Riq for help.

"The water's already hot and you don't need buckets," Riq said. "Most houses in our time have a heater inside, so there's always hot water when you turn on the tap."

"Oh." It was clear Bill didn't really follow. But he was trying. "What else is there in the future?"

Sera closed her eyes, not even knowing where to begin. Her world was just so different from Bill's on every conceivable level. But there was one other thing she wished she had even more than a hot shower: a phone to call Dak on to see if he was okay.

She tried to explain that to Bill. "Well, for one thing we have these things called cell phones. It's a way for you to talk to someone else who might be far away."

Bill's eyes grew wide. "How does that work?"

When she was six, Sera had built her own encrypted smartphone so that she and Dak could talk whenever they wanted. She started explaining the basics of the advanced mobile-phone system and digitized sampling, but Riq interrupted her.

"Ignore techno-geek over there. Basically everyone has a phone number—a series of numbers—that you plug into a keypad and, ta-da, you're talking to that person. I'm more of a language guy than a numbers guy, though, and since the numbers have letters associated

with them, that's how I memorize them. My phone number, for example, just happens to spell out the first ten
letters of *sesquipedalianist*." He paused before adding, "It
means I like big words."

Bill's brow was furrowed and he looked like he was
just about to ask a question when Sera bolted to her feet.

"That's it!" she said excitedly. She pressed her palms
against her forehead and groaned. "I can't believe I
didn't see it before. For the love of mincemeat! It was
so simple!"

Riq and Bill exchanged glances. "Uh, Sera?" Riq asked.
"What are you talking about?"

She knelt, using her finger to draw out a series of
numbers in the dirt. It didn't take long for Riq to figure
out what she was doing. When she hesitated, trying to
remember what came next, he helped to fill in the gaps.

"It's the series of numbers from the SQuare," she said.
"We thought it was some sort of bifid cipher but we
couldn't figure out what the key was." She began to draw
vertical lines to separate the numbers into pairs.

Below that she sketched the face of a phone keypad,
and that's when Riq groaned, "*Ooh*, I get it now. The first
number indicates which number on the keypad and the
second is the letter's position. So since *A*, *B*, and *C* are
all on the number two button, twenty-one becomes the
letter *A*. How did we miss that before?"

Sera was so elated that she couldn't help laughing
at the look of utter confusion on Bill's face. "Brint and
Mari wanted to ensure that no one from the past could

figure out the key to the cipher. What better way to do that than to use a gadget only someone from our time period would know?"

Riq was already matching letters to each pair of numbers so that 32 became *E* and 62 became *N*.

As he worked Bill reached over and ran the knuckles of his hand along the edge of Sera's jaw. Her breath caught and her cheeks blazed with heat.

"You'd smudged some dirt," he said softly.

She didn't know what to say and settled with, "Oh," which elicited a smile from him. That only made her neck burn hot as well and she wondered if Bill could see how furiously she was blushing in the dim light. She hoped not.

For his part, Riq seemed oblivious, his forehead scrunched up in concentration as he unraveled the message.

```
326274827332  744332413373433231  8121523274
7121734374  71322123323382535393
Ensure Siegfried Takes Paris Peacefully
```

All the blood heating Sera's cheeks drained as the message swirled through her mind. "If that's true . . ." She couldn't even finish the statement. She didn't want to give it voice, as if that could somehow make it real.

Riq didn't have such hesitation. He looked at her, his own face betraying fear. "Then we've definitely made things worse."

Dak was beginning to realize just how much trouble he'd gotten himself into. His arms were pinned behind him by the scarred Viking named Gorm, who looked a little too pleased to finally have Dak in his clutches.

Even though he had a good idea where he was being taken, his stomach twisted into knots as they approached the large structure dominating the far end of the camp. While most other Vikings slept out in the open or under simple A-frame tents, apparently Siegfried would do with nothing less than a wooden-framed hut.

Gorm thumped Dak forcefully on the back, shoving him so hard that he stumbled into the hovel. All conversation inside halted, though a few men snickered when Dak tripped and fell to his hands and knees.

Dak grimaced as the dirt floor scraped his palms. He felt the SQuare shift where it was jammed against his back and he froze, hoping it wouldn't slide free.

If Siegfried or any of the other men saw the SQuare, that would be the end of Dak and maybe even Sera and Riq as well. He couldn't risk it.

Slowly and carefully he lifted his head and looked around, using the movement to mask how he twisted his body to try and keep the SQuare in place. The structure had been built rapidly, and it showed in the crooked windows and uneven slant of the doorframe.

In the center blazed a fire, its smoke creating a thick layer of sludge along the ceiling as it struggled to find a way free through a hole in the roof. Carved earthen platforms topped with wooden boards and dingy rugs were built against the walls.

But what really drew Dak's attention were the men crouched around the fire, the flickering light casting shadows under their eyes. In the center of them sat Siegfried on the only stool in the room. Behind his shoulder a massive wooden shield hung from the wall, the SQ symbol emblazoned on it.

He looked over Dak's head to where Gorm the Time Warden stood in the door. "This doesn't look like dinner," he said, raising one eyebrow.

It didn't escape Dak's notice that this was the second time in two days someone had discussed eating him. He was really beginning to hate the ninth century.

15

The Blood Eagle

DAK TRIED to call as little attention to himself as possible, which wasn't very easy when every eye in the room was focused on him.

"I found him sabotaging one of the ships." Gorm walked farther into the room until he was towering over Dak. "If it weren't for this boy, our plan to burn the bridge would have worked and we'd be in the city already."

This seemed to pique Siegfried's interest. He leaned forward, causing his stool to groan and crack in protest. For several moments, the Viking chieftain examined Dak until Dak couldn't take it anymore, and he started to squirm.

"I just tripped." Dak was dismayed at how scared and high-pitched his voice sounded. He scowled, trying to regain a little control of the situation. "If this guy" — he jerked a finger over his shoulder in the general direction of the Time Warden — "had better control of his boat, everything would have worked out fine."

Siegfried frowned and sent a questioning glance at Gorm, who quickly responded, "He may have tripped, but he also cut a hole in the hull with an axe."

Dak let out a long exhale. There really was no explanation he could give for that, but he still tried. "I thought the fire needed ventilation?"

One of the other men around the fire chuckled and quickly covered it by launching into a bout of coughing.

"You look familiar," Siegfried prodded.

Dak swallowed, the sound so loud he was pretty sure the entire room heard. "I was your standard-bearer yesterday at the wall," he offered.

Siegfried shook his head. "From somewhere else." He squinted at Dak, trying to place him.

"He was with the translator in the cathedral," Gorm offered. "The boy who spoke the Danish tongue as well as Latin and French."

The grin that spread across Siegfried's face did nothing to calm Dak's fears. In fact, it made his blood run icy cold. There was nothing pleasant in the man's expression, just pure malice.

What Gorm said next only made things worse. "He's been working to sabotage your efforts. Who knows how many of our men have fallen because of him."

That was going too far. Dak leapt to his feet. "It's not true," he shouted. "If it weren't for me, more men would have been crushed or burned. I saved them!"

There were a few murmurs around the fire, but no one came to Dak's defense—even though he recognized some of the men as ones who only the night before had been clapping him on the back in thanks.

Siegfried stood as well and came around the fire until he was towering over Dak. He smelled like old clotted cheese and his hands bunched into meaty fists. "Where are you from, boy?"

Dak opened his mouth to answer, but then realized that he couldn't—Pennsylvania didn't even exist yet. It was that slight hesitation that caused Siegfried's eyes to gleam.

"How old are you?" Siegfried pressed.

Dak answered easily: "Eleven."

"When were you born?"

The room was silent as Dak ran the calculation through his head in a panic. He'd never been one for numbers, and in the time it took for him to subtract eleven from 885, he'd confirmed Siegfried's and the Time Warden's suspicions.

"I-I'm not good with math," he offered, but even he heard how lame the excuse was.

Siegfried leaned in so close that Dak could smell the sourness of his breath. It was even worse than Vígi's, if that was possible.

"You and I both know who you really are," Siegfried growled. The other Vikings in the room strained to listen in but Siegfried kept his voice low enough that only Dak could hear over the popping of the fire.

Panic flared in Dak's stomach and the adrenaline pumping through his veins screamed at him to run.

He was in way over his head. The Viking laid a heavy hand on Dak's shoulder as if sensing the direction of his thoughts.

"You Hystorians have tried to stop us before but you underestimate our might and dedication to the cause."

Dak tried to protest and feign ignorance; it was his only option. "I don't know what you're talking about."

Siegfried's fingers tightened on Dak's shoulder until he felt as though the Viking might rip his arm from his body. Sweat trailed down Dak's back and he felt it pooling against the SQuare, causing it to shift.

Not now, he thought fiercely. Of course, that just caused him to sweat even more, which wasn't helping matters.

"You Hystorians are so easy to outsmart." Siegfried's eyes gleamed. "You're always so obsessed with playing by the rules. That will always be your downfall."

Dak tried to look brave. "At least we have honor," he retorted.

This only caused the Viking to tilt his head back with bone-shaking laughter that he cut off abruptly. He grabbed Dak's chin between his finger and thumb so tightly that Dak's eyes watered.

"I want you to hand over whatever it is that's letting you sail through time," he growled. "Nothing will get in the way of my power." As if to emphasize his point he shook Dak roughly.

The SQuare slipped a little more so that it was now slowly sliding down his leg in his pants. Dak flexed his leg and squeezed, desperately trying to keep the device from dropping to the ground.

"I don't know —" Dak started, but he was interrupted when Siegfried began shaking him even more. The SQuare caught behind his knee and he was certain that if anyone looked they'd see the shape of the device outlined against his pant leg.

Dak quickly shifted tactics. "I don't have it," he blurted out.

This stopped the shaking. "Get it," Siegfried barked.

"I can't," Dak explained. "It's inside the city walls."

Siegfried pushed Dak with a roar. Dak crumpled to the floor, using the motion to yank the SQuare from his pants and shove it back under his waistband. When he looked up all eyes were still on Siegfried except for one pair on the far side of the room. It was Rollo, his expression trained on Dak with interest.

Dak knew right away the Viking had seen the SQuare. He waited for the large man to sound some sort of alarm or bring it to Siegfried's attention but instead he remained silent, his focus glued on Dak's every move.

Siegfried crouched, drawing Dak forward by his tunic. "You'll get me that device and I'll make yours a quick death. Defy me, and you, as well as your friends, will have the blood eagle just like Ivar the Boneless gave to Ælla of Northumbria."

Dak frowned, his confusion evident. "Blood eagle?"

Gorm grinned, his teeth gleaming in anticipation. "We'll slice open your back. Cut your ribs, one by one, and break them open to look like the bloody wings of an eagle. Then we pull out your lungs and watch them flutter. When we get bored with that, we'll rip out your lungs and pour salt on all the wounds. Don't worry about missing out—you'll be alive and screaming through most of it."

16

Connections from Long Ago

DAK TUGGED again on the bars to his tiny cage, hoping that perhaps in the last five minutes they'd grown loose, but nothing budged. It was like being in the brig of the *Santa María* all over again except this time he was freezing and alone.

Dak was beginning to accept that history could kind of stink.

He'd been so sure that his knowledge would keep them all safe. And now look at him: waiting in a cage for a Viking chieftain to grow tired of him and toss him to the wolves.

As if just thinking the word *wolf* was enough to cause one to materialize, Dak heard a soft whining and then the brush of a cold nose against his knuckles. He squinted his eyes in the darkness to find Vígi standing by his cage, her ears pinned back in worry.

She paced around the cage restlessly, stopping every now and again to nudge his hand. He tried to pet her but could only manage to draw two fingers along the ridge of her snout.

"It's okay, girl," he whispered. He was surprised to hear his voice quaver a bit. He was glad that at least some living being cared about what happened to him.

A large form lumbered out of the darkness, rain dripping from his metal helmet and causing his thick cloak to hang limp and heavy from his shoulders. Dak squinted, trying to make out who it was.

"Well," the Viking said, striding toward the cage. Vígi's tail thumped the ground as he neared. "You do keep surprising me."

Dak recognized the voice before he saw the face: It was Rollo. The giant tugged on the bars of the cage, bending them open as though they were strings of cheese, and leaned his head in. "Now, you want to tell me what that contraption jammed down your pants is?"

Dak was totally busted. He squirmed in his cage, but that didn't deter Rollo, who merely reached in and plucked the SQuare from behind Dak's back. His finger must have brushed the ON switch, because it chirped to life with a bright light.

Rollo squealed in surprise, holding the SQuare away from his body as though it were some sort of poisonous bug that was crawling up his arm.

"Careful!" Dak cried. "Uh, please."

"What is this thing?" Rollo asked, his eyes illuminated with wonder and by the light of the screen. Vígi bared her teeth in a growl, the hair between her shoulder blades standing on end so that she looked like a buffalo calf.

It was time for Dak to admit that he'd royally messed up. His cover was blown; no lie could dig him out of this hole. And he couldn't fight the man either. Rollo could fell Dak with the flick of a finger. Plus, he was pretty sure that even though Vígi seemed to like him, the moment Dak threatened her master it would be all over for him.

"Back by the fire," Rollo said, his gaze still riveted by the glowing screen, "you couldn't say what year you were born."

Dak felt his cheeks warm. He was a genius with history and dates; that he couldn't answer that one simple question was a massive source of embarrassment.

He fumbled for an excuse. "I get nervous in front of, uh, chieftains."

Rollo waved his words from the air. "It's not me you have to worry about with this lot," he said. "I'll follow Siegfried when it's in my best interest, but that doesn't mean I support him in all endeavors, if you know what I mean."

Dak wasn't sure that he did and so he stayed silent.

The SQuare's screen went dark and Rollo sighed with dismay. Vígi relaxed, leaning all her weight against Dak's cage. Dak absently scratched at her ears and she grunted contentedly.

"My great-grandfather was one of the men to sack Lindisfarne Priory almost a century ago. It's true that Norsemen can be a dangerous lot who go off on voyages simply for the fighting and pillaging, but my great-grandfather was not a violent man. He was simply looking for someplace to settle down and start a farm with his wife."

He smoothed his palm across the screen of the SQuare over and over again but he seemed lost in thought. "He told my father that he was surprised at how bloodthirsty the men were that day—more so than he'd ever seen before. He'd been hearing rumors about a new allegiance among several of them, some sort of quest for power that caused them to burn the Priory and kill everyone on the island."

Dak thought of Siegfried and Gorm, and the calculated coldness of their eyes. He had no doubt that they and their ancestors could be a ruthless lot.

"My great-grandfather tried to avoid most of the pillaging, but as he was exploring the lower passages of the Priory he came upon a young monk who was trying to hide a few books. As soon as he saw my great-grandfather, the monk threw himself on his knees and begged for mercy."

Vígi shifted, shoving her head farther into the cage, and Dak realized he'd stopped petting her. He was holding his breath, afraid of what Rollo might say next.

It occurred to Dak that he liked the giant and didn't want anything to ruin that feeling.

Rollo continued with his story. "The chieftains leading the raid had made it clear that everyone on the island must die. But when my great-grandfather drew his sword, he hesitated. The monk began to tell him about a group of scholars called the Hystorians whose job was to protect the past, present, and future. He said that if he died, a group of wicked men would gain boundless power that would eventually destroy the world."

Dak swallowed when Rollo hesitated. "What did he do?"

Rollo handed Dak the SQuare. "He let the monk go free. And he told my grandfather, who told my father, who told me what he learned in the Priory that day: that there are forces in the world greater than we can understand, and if we ever had the opportunity to grant mercy where it felt warranted we should do so without hesitation."

With a grunt, Rollo rose to his towering height and extended a hand toward Dak. "He taught me to be on the lookout for the extraordinary and to protect it. I'm pretty sure he was talking about you."

It had rained throughout the night, and Sera had watched it for hours. She'd lost track of Bill, and now she had an unfounded fear that if she were to doze off, Riq would disappear, too.

A faint light began to seep along the horizon, struggling through the clouds, and church bells rang from not far away. She'd stayed up all night. And now it wouldn't be long before the fighting commenced once again.

Riq peered out the window, his face twisting into resignation at the dreariness of the morning. He turned to her, leaning back against the rough stone wall and crossing one foot over the other. "What's the plan, then?"

Sera had never considered herself any kind of leader before. But now it seemed Riq was looking to her for guidance. And why not? This entire mission had gone off the rails, with every move they made only causing things to get worse. She dreaded imagining about how their actions had already impacted the future.

"Well, we botched the negotiation. If we could have made the Parisians and Vikings see eye-to-eye, maybe convinced Siegfried not to sack the city at all, then maybe he would have settled here and never gone on to Normandy, and his great-great-great-grandson Bill Helm might have been a farmer instead of a vanquisher."

"Sorry." Riq grimaced, as he'd been the one who'd mistranslated the discussion between the Vikings and Bishop Gauzelin the first morning the Vikings came into Paris. If they'd been able to decipher the code on the SQuare before leaping into action, they might have already fixed the Break and warped on to the next. And Dak might still be—

Sera waved a hand in the air. "What's done is done and can't be undone." She paused. "Well, I mean *technically* it could be undone as we could go back through time, but it can't be undone without causing more problems. The Wellsian radiation alone would—"

Riq was giving her that look that meant what she was saying was over his head. She cleared her throat. "Anyway, so, we've already mucked things up, but that doesn't mean we can't make it right. I still think our plan of keeping the Vikings at bay for as long as possible is a good one. At the end of the day we need to limit Siegfried's power one way or another. And if the Franks win, we've done that. According to Bill, Bishop Gauzelin and Count Odo have sent for reinforcements from the king, Charles the Fat. Now it's just a matter of holding out and waiting for help."

"So what do we do in the meantime?" Riq asked.

Sera tried to grin but she was pretty sure it looked more like a grimace. "We help. We keep Paris from falling to the Vikings. And if Dak doesn't make it back to us" — she took a deep breath — "then we go after him ourselves."

17

Berserkergang

OF ALL the experiences Dak had imagined having on
his travels, this wasn't one of them. Under Rollo's super-
vision, he'd stripped off his shirt and was only allowed
to keep his pants on so that he could hide the SQuare.

Most of the men surrounding them, preparing for the
first of the morning battles, were completely naked with
mud smeared across their bodies. If there was anything
they all had in common it was that they were horrifically
ugly with noses that had been broken too many times
to have any cartilage or bone left, and thick eyebrows
that connected across their foreheads.

A bit of panic churned in Dak's stomach. No matter
what Rollo insisted, there was no way Dak was going to
pass as one of these men. His entire body was the size
of one of their legs!

"This isn't going to work," he whispered to Rollo.
The giant merely grunted in reply, motioning for Dak to
smear more mud across his bare chest. Dak continued
to sneak glances at those around him.

"So, you're saying I don't get any kind of armor?" Dak asked as Rollo pulled a wolf skin around his shoulders so that the head of the wolf rested on top of Dak's own.

"The spirit of this animal will protect you," Rollo answered, completely serious.

Dak wanted to say, "Yeah, because it worked so well for the animal," but he kept that thought to himself.

"You know you're insane, right?" Dak asked instead.

Rollo heaved a sigh. "I told you, Siegfried's men are already searching the camp for you. If you have any chance of getting back inside the city to your friends, it's in going with the first wave of battle. And that means becoming *berserkr*."

A hulk of a man, completely naked except for a bear skin draped over his shoulders, walked through the group, offering each a flagon of what smelled like wine or some other kind of fermented fruit.

Dak braced himself when it came to be his turn, expecting the man to either burst out laughing or become enraged and pull his limbs apart with his bare hands. But the brute hardly seemed to notice Dak, just handed him a flagon and continued on.

Curious, Dak raised it to his lips only to find his hands empty. Rollo scowled at him as he poured the contents of the flagon onto the ground. "This isn't for boys," he said, which made Dak all bristly . . . until he realized what the drink was doing to the men around him.

One by one they began to shiver, their teeth (those who still had them) clacking together noisily. Sure it was cold outside and most of the men were naked and wet from the rain, but they were such brutes of men that Dak assumed they'd be immune to chilly weather.

Rollo leaned over and whispered into Dak's ear. "Once the *berserkergang* begins, stay to the left and toward the back. Whatever you do, don't get between a *berserkr* and the enemy."

Dak nodded, his stomach sour with anticipation and worry. The more he thought about Rollo's plan, the less confident he felt. There was no way this was going to work. "Maybe we should just take our chances with—"

Rollo ignored him and instead handed Dak an axe like the one he'd had before. "Let them do the fighting. When they punch through the wall of the fortification, that's when you make your move."

"How do you know they'll breach the city?" Dak asked, his panic increasing exponentially as he thought about Sera and Riq, not to mention their mission of keeping Siegfried out of Paris.

Rollo smiled and for a brief moment Dak saw the Viking in him—that part that drove him from home toward battle after battle. It caused the hair to raise along his arms. "No one can stand against the *berserkergang*," he said.

Church bells rang in the distance, waking the fortified city for another day of battle. Dak stared across the expanse toward the river. Already he could see men patrolling the ramparts. Between here and there Vikings were attempting to roll siege engines across the bumpy ground closer to the tower.

"That's the problem," he murmured. The only way

for him to get back to Sera and Riq was for Paris to fall. But if Paris fell, they'd fail at fixing the Break.

He didn't know what to do. Everything he knew about history had already changed. There was no mental guidebook he could consult, no set of facts he could rely on to figure out what the best move would be.

"Maybe—" he started, but his voice was swallowed by the horns from the Viking camp. He was running out of time. His mind raced. There had to be a way to fix this Break, some detail he was missing. He scoured through various historical events in his head, tilting and turning them for any weakness.

A thought came to him. As more and more horns began to blast he clutched Rollo's arm. "There's one other thing you can do to help," he shouted. Rollo frowned; it was clear he couldn't hear him.

As if the horns had triggered it, the *berserkrs* around him stopped chattering as their faces turned a dark purple, their cheeks swelling as though they'd swallowed some sort of poison. Their already hideous faces became the masks of monsters.

Dak motioned furiously for Rollo to lean closer and then he shouted instructions into his ear. When he was done, Rollo straightened and gave a nod.

And then, with a massive roar of rage, the *berserker-gang* began. Rollo slapped Dak on the back, shoving him toward the group. "Good-bye, friend," he said. Vígi whined, straining at the frayed leash holding her by Rollo's side.

Dak nodded his thanks and began to run.

Their situation was so much worse than Sera had thought, she realized as she stood with Riq on the ramparts of the wall ringing the Île de la Cité. The rains during the night had led to flooding, which wasn't helped by all the debris the Vikings had spent the day before throwing into the river. That, coupled with the half-sunk/half-burned Viking ships, meant that an enormous amount of strain was being put on the already damaged bridge. And if the bridge fell, the Vikings would finally be able to surround Paris.

Already she could hear the supports of the bridge groaning. Parisians were trying to relieve the pressure by prying loose some of the larger obstacles but the bridge was built so low to the water that nothing was working.

It didn't help matters that it was still pouring, rain turning everything into a sodden mess. She could see on the faces around her that the Franks were ready to give up.

They couldn't allow that to happen.

From across the river she heard horns wail and men scream with rage. It reminded her of their first day, the moment just after they'd warped when the ground shook with the stampede of the massive Viking army.

That morning Siegfried had pulled most of his men back at the last minute, only wanting to show the Franks the force of his might.

Today the Parisians wouldn't be so lucky.

"Maybe you should take the Ring and get someplace safer," Riq suggested.

Sera shook her head. "We're in this together," she told him but as soon as the words left her mouth she was hit with a bout of dizziness. Her stomach lurched and she stumbled. If it weren't for Riq grabbing hold of her, she would have fallen.

She squeezed her eyes shut but that didn't stop the feeling that something was horribly off about the world. The words she'd just uttered, "We're in this together," echoed through her head again and again, and her heart ached with each incantation.

Phantom hands cupped her cheeks; a face like her own peered down at her with eyes brimming with love. She was warm and safe and loved and cherished.

And then it was gone, but Sera couldn't bear to open her eyes and return to the harshness of their reality. She wanted to live inside the Remnant.

"It's okay," Riq was murmuring, but she didn't believe him. It had never been okay.

Riq maneuvered her until she was sitting with her back against one of the crenellations and he pushed her head between her knees so that she could catch her breath and keep the world from spinning.

He didn't have to ask her what had happened. It was clear from his expression that he understood. "We have to fix this Break," she finally said when she'd caught her breath. "It's the only way to stop the Remnants. I don't know if I can take them any longer."

"We will," Riq promised, his hand warm against her back. Sera marveled at how not too long ago she'd viewed Riq as an annoying third wheel who did nothing but cause trouble. Now she realized she'd almost call him a friend.

"Thanks," she murmured.

He nodded, the gesture growing still as he looked over her shoulder out toward the river and the fields beyond. His eyes widened as an expression of horror crossed his face.

"What?" Sera demanded. She shifted to her knees. Riq tried to keep her from looking, but she finally dodged around him until she could see what had caused him such fear.

A band of naked men was sprinting across the field, furs of various animals trailing from their shoulders and gleaming weapons waving over their heads. They screamed and roared, their faces purple. Aghast, she averted her eyes . . . and that's when she saw Dak at the edge of the pack, axe raised in the air as he ran at full speed toward the fortified walls.

18

Rallying the Troops

SERA RACED down the ladders and to the bridge. Waves crashed over the sides, making the stone surface dangerously slick. The north tower on the mainland looked very far away, but that didn't stop her. Riq called after her, but she didn't wait for him to catch up. More than once she slipped and fell, wincing as she scraped her palms and skinned her knees.

Over the roar of the rising river she heard the sound of battle just beginning. Through the gaps in the north tower's metal gate she caught glimpses of men fighting. She clenched her hands into fists, refusing to even consider that she might be too late.

She had to make it to the tower. She had to keep the archers from taking aim at her best friend. She had to find a way to get Dak back safely.

She didn't want to think about the consequences if she failed.

Stones fell from the sky, clattering around her: the first wave of assaults from the Viking siege engines. A few pebbles struck her shoulder and a massive boulder landed two inches to her left, almost crushing her toes.

She was just approaching the entrance to the tower when Riq barreled into her, shoving her to safety. Behind them arrows whizzed and pots of flaming oil exploded. A few flames sputtered around their feet and Riq leapt to stomp them out.

They stared at each other for a second, trying to catch their breath, both aware that if they'd been any slower they probably wouldn't have made it without catching fire or getting impaled. As it was, the bridge was already beginning to crumble under the force of the swollen river and the crash of falling debris.

"If the bridge goes, we'll be stuck on the wrong side of the river!" Riq shouted.

"We have to," Sera responded. "For Dak."

Riq nodded and pulled Sera to her feet. Together they raced through the tower. From above they heard the shouts of soldiers trying to fight through bouts of punishing rain.

They'd just started up a set of stone stairs when the wall to their right began to tremble. At first Sera only felt a series of vibrations but soon enough they were strong enough to jolt her off balance. Stones shook loose, pebbles falling from the ceiling.

Men began to stream down from above, their swords drawn and their faces vivid with panic. "Run!" the soldier in the lead shouted. "They're about to breach!" They raced back toward the fortified island.

Riq grabbed Sera by the wrist and began to drag her across the bridge. She dug in her heels.

"What are you doing?" Riq asked, aghast.

"If they breach, we fail," she said softly.

"If we die, any hope of avoiding the Cataclysm dissolves."

They looked at each other as soldiers streamed past them. One man made it only three steps along the bridge before being struck by an arrow. He fell to his knees and collapsed, his sword clattering from his grasp.

There was another loud thud and the ground jolted under their feet, causing Sera to stumble. A tremendous cracking sound boomed as fissures raced through the outer wall of the tower. Streaks of watery morning light began to filter through, accompanied by the sound of Vikings raging.

The tower wall was crumbling.

Sera looked back at the fortified island through the rain. Soldiers ringed the ramparts, their bows raised as they let loose arrow after arrow, so fast their movements were a blur.

She slipped her hand into the sack on her belt. Her fingers tightened around the Infinity Ring, hidden inside. She knew Riq was right; it was smarter for them to retreat.

But Sera was tired of always having to make the smart choices. Just this once, she wanted to make the bold one and follow her gut.

Everything around her trembled and strained, the tower groaning under the onslaught of siege engines. As the first chunk fell free Sera dashed toward the fallen soldier on the bridge and snatched up his sword.

Riq was so stunned he didn't move to stop her. With a crashing boom, a break opened in the wall, the last bit of defense between the Vikings and the Franks crumbling. Even though her heart pounded ferociously and her hands trembled, she refused to let fear make her hesitate.

As soon as the dust cleared from the collapsed wall, Sera leapt into the breach with the sword held high. Her gaze skimmed over the mass of Viking warriors racing toward her clad only in the skins of animals until she spotted Dak.

"Go!" she screamed at him. "Go!"

The moment Dak saw Sera step from the rubble of the broken wall waving a massive sword over her head Dak thought, *She's gone completely insane.* Then he started running faster.

All around him *berserkrs* screamed and bellowed, their faces monstrous masks of rage. Some were clearly injured, arrows piercing arms or chests, but they seemed not to notice or slow. There would be no reasoning, no calling them back. And they were all running straight for Sera and the gap in the tower.

She stood on the pile of rubble, her sword held high in such a way that it gleamed in the damp morning. She looked bold and fierce — unlike the science geek who'd been his best friend for years.

She looks like she's about to get herself killed. Blood roared in Dak's ears at the thought, making his feet pound faster than he thought was possible.

He tried waving his arms, calling for her to fall back, but his voice was lost in the din of the battlefield.

And then a curious thing happened. Soldiers began to pour from the breach behind Sera, men in armor with swords and axes and spears and arrows. They streamed around Sera as though she were rallying them with a battle cry.

"For Lutetia!" they shouted, paying homage to the old Roman name for Paris as they raced into the fray.

For an instant the *berserkrs* hesitated, faced with this new approaching army. Dak himself was so distracted by the sight of Sera that he didn't notice the boy racing at him until it was too late. He tackled Dak, slamming him to the ground. Dak rolled, struggling to get a better grip on his axe as the two of them tussled for control of the weapon.

Dak was not exactly a seasoned warrior, but he still managed to gain the advantage on his opponent, twisting until he was kneeling on his chest. Dak was just about to clobber the boy over his head with the axe handle when he held up his empty hands and gasped: "Wait! I'm with Sera!"

The axe hovered inches from the boy's head. The adrenaline coursing through Dak's body urged him to strike fast and hard, but his brain was screaming at him to stop and listen.

With a great deal of effort, he held still, hands

trembling from the rush of battle. "Prove it," he growled, surprised at how raw and angry his voice sounded.

"My name is Billfrith," he said. "I'm a . . . a . . ." He seemed to hesitate over the word and then leaned forward and whispered, "Hystorian."

Dak blinked back his surprise and then rolled from the boy, giving him a chance to breathe. "I thought you'd be older."

Billfrith twisted his lips. "Well, imagine my surprise when I realized the fate of the world rested in the hands of kids."

"Hey," Dak countered. "We haven't screwed it up yet, have we?"

The other boy declined to respond to that and instead rose to his feet, tugging Dak up after him. "I'd love to sit and chat about the effectiveness of your efforts, but if you haven't noticed we're sitting in the middle of a battlefield. Perhaps we could find someplace less deadly to catch up." An arrow pierced the ground between them. "Now would be a good time to start running."

19

The Reunion

SERA STOOD stunned as Frankish troops streamed around her, racing out toward the battlefield with weapons drawn and cries of victory on their lips. Several of them nodded to her as they ran past, as though she were somehow responsible for this turn of events.

Surrounded by the crowd of soldiers, she lost track of Dak. The adrenaline rush of the last several moments began to dim, quickly replaced with a rising tide of panic.

Riq appeared by her side and she clutched his arm. "Where's Dak?!" she asked.

"This way," he answered, and he took off running across the battlefield. Sera followed. For the time being, both sides had halted the flow of arrows, the armies so jumbled it was impossible to let loose anything and not endanger their own men.

Sera and Riq took advantage of this lull, dodging past groups of sparring warriors. She cringed as blade met blade and metal sliced through leather. The Viking *berserkrs* lived up to their name, a sheen of madness glazing over their eyes as they fought with a rage that seemed incomprehensible.

Riq led her toward a large stone church on the edge of the battlefield, just out of range of the fighting. Sera caught a glimpse of two tall towers bookending a wall set with arched windows before they hurried inside.

It was the smell that did it to her. She'd been expecting a normal church, the dusty scent of stones mixed with the lingering hint of incense. What greeted her was the stench of a barnyard: wet wool, damp hay, and the close quarters of too many animals.

The Remnant slammed into her, causing her to stumble. She was reminded of the abandoned barn on the edge of her uncle's property and hit with the sense that this is what it should smell like.

She swore she could feel someone taking her hand and gliding it along the flank of a horse, patiently teaching her how to care for the animal after a wild ride through the fresh grass.

She sucked in a gasp, dizziness spiraling through her. Strong hands gripped her shoulders, easing her to the ground.

When she was able to open her eyes she found Riq kneeling in front of her. "Sera?" he whispered.

She blinked, trying to gather her thoughts and stop the churning in her stomach. "I . . . I'm okay."

It was clear from Riq's face that he knew she was lying. Even so, he didn't press her on it. Instead he helped her to her feet and ushered her from the vestibule into the church proper.

Any pews that once existed had been stripped out or arranged to make crude pens for the slew of animals housed inside. But that's not what drew Sera's attention.

"Dak!" she cried out, and then she was running toward her best friend.

Dak didn't admit it out loud, but he couldn't have been happier to see Sera, and even Riq, running into the church. He allowed Sera to hug him, relieved to see his best friend again.

They all started talking at once, swapping stories about what they'd been through over the past few days, but their reunion was cut short by Billfrith. He dashed in from where he'd been keeping watch in the bell tower. "Sorry, but we don't have time for a happy reunion," he said, out of breath. "A band of Vikings is headed this way, and they don't look too pleased."

"Bill!" Sera said in surprise. Dak watched with interest as her cheeks colored. "You're safe."

The Hystorian smiled shyly back at her and Dak snickered, a sound he cut off instantly when faced with a glare from Sera. He cleared his throat, but his shoulders still lurched a bit with unspent laughter.

"I wouldn't be the one laughing, wolf boy," Riq muttered under his breath and now it was Dak's turn to blush, remembering that he was basically half-naked with a wolf pelt slung from his shoulders.

"There's no time," Bill insisted. Even as he said the words, a loud crash rang out from the front of the church. "I've barred the door, but it won't hold for long."

He turned to Dak. "Do you have the SQuare?" Dak nodded, pulling it free. "And you have the Ring?" Bill asked Sera. She pulled it out but didn't make any moves to start programming it.

"We haven't fixed the Break yet," she protested.

Bill stepped toward her and placed his hand on her shoulder. "Your safety is more important," he said softly.

Sera shook her head and turned to Dak. "We unraveled the code after you left. It said that we were supposed to let Siegfried take the city peacefully. Riq and I figure that the Hystorians speculated that Siegfried would settle here, never extending his power, never heading to Normandy at all."

Riq supplied the conclusion Sera hadn't. "It means we messed up by prodding the Franks to fight."

Dak thought through the implications of that. He ran through various scenarios, playing out the effects of their actions through history like an intricate chess game. "But as long as we keep the Vikings from Normandy, we should be cool, right?" he concluded.

Riq and Sera exchanged a glance and a shrug.

"I mean, really all we're doing is preventing the SQ from establishing themselves in Normandy. And if the Vikings never settle there, we'll have done that."

"I guess," Sera agreed. "But how can we do that?"

Dak grinned. "I've taken care of everything."

They heard another boom and the cracking of wood against stone. A familiar dog came loping into view from the back of the church. When she reached Dak she reared on her hind legs to place her front paws on his shoulders. Vígi gave his face a very wet lick and Dak gagged at the smell.

Behind her ambled Rollo, each footfall the sound of thunder. Sera, Riq, and Bill all drew weapons although their faces paled.

"Your friend is right," Rollo boomed. "I'll keep Siegfried and the others from Normandy if that's what needs to happen. I hear Burgundy is nice this time of year and that King Charles the Fat has a fondness for paying large fees to those who help him quell uprisings. Nothing a man like Siegfried likes better than a hefty purse of silver!"

Sera glanced at Dak, her eyes huge. "He's with you?" she mouthed. Dak grinned.

"That's really all we had to do?" Riq asked, his suspicion evident.

Rollo glanced over his shoulder toward the front of the church. "Well, that and get out of here as fast as possible. In about three minutes Siegfried's men are coming in here after you. I can do a better job of barring the door, but if it didn't keep me out you can bet they'll get in eventually."

Dak turned to Sera. "You ready?" he asked, holding out the SQuare. She glanced at Bill and swallowed, finally nodding.

"Where to?" she asked.

Riq took the SQuare and called up the information on the third Break. He traced his fingers lightly over a pattern of circles, his forehead furrowing.

Around them animals shifted in their makeshift stalls, a few sheep bleating their unease.

It had never taken the older boy this long to piece together a The Art of Memory puzzle. Previously, he'd only had to glimpse the pattern to ascertain the time and place of the next Break that needed to be fixed.

"We have to hurry," Dak stressed. He was about to say more when Sera placed her hand on his arm, stopping him. The expression on her face was enough for Dak to know she wanted him to shut up and let Riq work.

Dak scowled—since when had Sera stood up for Riq over him?

He had certainly missed a lot in the past few days.

"I've got it!" Riq shouted. He tilted the screen to show the two of them, but it only looked like a random swirling pattern to Dak. He glanced at Sera, wondering if she saw something he didn't, but she appeared just as confused.

"Washington, DC—former capital of the United States, in 1814. Looks like we're headed to the War of 1812," Riq explained.

A few days ago Dak would have been clapping his hands together with glee over the prospect of witnessing another battlefield firsthand. He'd spent so many afternoons daydreaming about what those places had been like in the heat of battle.

But he only sighed. "Another war," he said dryly. "Awesome."

A Hasty Retreat

SERA FOCUSED on her fingers flying over the controls of the Infinity Ring because that way she didn't have to look at Bill. Every time she glanced over at him her stomach fluttered. To calm herself down she ran differential equations through her head, but it didn't seem to work the way it usually did.

"Oh, for the love of mincemeat," she muttered, angry at herself for spending the last few moments she had in the year 885 avoiding the fact that she'd gone and gotten a crush on the Hystorian.

As if he knew she was thinking of him, he slid down the wall to sit next to her where she'd found a quiet nook to program the Ring. Her fingers fumbled over the controls.

It didn't help that Dak and Riq kept peeking around the corner at her anxiously while the giant Viking paced back and forth, swinging his axe through the air.

And yet if Sera was honest with herself, she didn't want to go. Not yet. She cleared her throat, trying to think of something to say.

"That looks complicated," Bill said, staring at the Ring. She only nodded in response.

"Dak said you were the one to make it work." He ran his fingers through his dark hair and Sera wondered if he was as nervous as she felt. "That's pretty impressive."

"Thanks." Sera's fingers stilled on the controls.

Bill stared at the Ring. "I guess that means it's all programmed and you're ready to go?"

Was it just Sera or was there a hint of regret in his voice? She took a chance with her answer and told him the truth. "I finished programming it a couple of minutes ago."

"Then why . . . ?" Bill's face scrunched in confusion and then he seemed to understand what she was saying. That she'd pretended to keep working on the Infinity Ring to buy more time because she didn't want to leave. "Oh!"

Sera had faced down a horde of *berserkrs* but turning toward Bill in that moment was one of the hardest things she'd done. "I wish you could go with us," she murmured. She felt her cheeks blaze hot, but that was okay because she was pretty sure Bill was blushing, too.

He laid his hand on where hers gripped the Infinity Ring. "Me, too. But you know better than anyone what it means to be a Hystorian: My job is to stay behind and record what I know for future Hystorians. If I warp away with you, then the truth of what happened here will be lost."

The thing was, Sera understood what he was saying and yet she still prickled at it. She remembered what Riq had said earlier about his parents, how being a Hystorian took over your life. She tried not to resent it. She knew how important their mission was—that the fate of the world rested with them—but that didn't mean it didn't stink sometimes.

"So what now?" she whispered.

He grinned and started to lean toward her, one of his hands reaching out. Her heart began to pound so loudly it drowned out the Vikings trying to force their way inside. "We enjoy the time we have left," he offered.

Sera's thoughts went in a thousand different directions at once as Bill came closer, wondering what was going to happen next. But it didn't matter because right then Dak came around the corner, invading their bubble of privacy.

"Hey, did you know there's an actual saint buried here? They say a saint's bones never rot and instead emit a sweet odor, but when I took a whiff I didn't notice anything and it sure isn't doing a thing to cover up the stench of all those animals. . . ." Dak's voice trailed off when he realized he'd just interrupted something.

"In fact, I think that might be the woman who single-handedly rallied Paris against Attila and the Huns in 451. So," Dak continued as if he could salvage the situation, "that's pretty cool. I know how you like the stories about strong women from the past."

"Spare me the history lesson," Sera grumbled.

It didn't matter anyway. They were interrupted by a massive shattering and a series of shouts as Siegfried and his men stormed into the church.

Dak's world exploded into chaos.

"Stop them!" Siegfried roared at his men. Rollo stood between them, his sword, *Kettlingr,* raised. Beside him Vígi growled, baring her teeth as the hair rose along her back.

"Go!" Rollo shouted at them.

"But aren't you supposed to be on the same side as him?" Dak asked, indicating the enraged Siegfried. He knew that for their plan to work Rollo had to convince the other Vikings to leave Normandy alone, and he was afraid that this would ruin everything.

Rollo just smiled. "Vikings like Siegfried love to fight. Tomorrow he'll be thanking me for getting his blood moving. Now go!"

Dak didn't need to be told twice. But he also knew how stupid it would be for the three of them to warp away in front of prying eyes. He grabbed Sera and Riq, and pulled them deeper into the church and around behind a pen of squealing pigs.

"Is it programmed?" Dak pointed at the Infinity Ring still clutched in Sera's grasp. Footsteps pounded through the nave of the church, Vikings shoving cows and sheep out of the way as they searched for the three time travelers.

"Y-yes," she stammered. She glanced at Bill, her face twisted with confusion and regret.

"Let's get out of here!" Dak shouted. He waited for Sera to do whatever it was that would warp them away from 885 France. Nothing happened. The sound of enraged Vikings drew closer and closer. He caught glimpses of Rollo defending himself against four men at once while Vígi cornered two more.

It wasn't until he saw Bill holding Sera's hand that Dak realized what was causing the delay. "You're going to have to let her go," he said. "Unless you want to hitch a ride to 1814."

"Sera," Riq prodded, and Dak noticed that the voice he used with her was a lot softer than the one he used with him.

For a moment Sera stared at Bill and Bill stared back. Dak didn't even begin to wonder what wordless exchange was going on between them. He huffed with impatience and finally reached for the Ring. "If you're not going to do it, I will."

Sera's expression turned ferocious. It was actually pretty cool — he'd never seen her so angry (except for that one time they went to a paper presentation on proton decay in particle physics and the guy kept mixing up his quarks). But he'd much prefer it if her newfound ire weren't directed at him.

She was forced to drop Bill's hand to fight for control of the Ring. It was at that moment, while Dak and Sera were both distracted, that a familiar face stepped from the shadows in the back of the church, his bow held straight in front of him, string pulled taut.

Grom.

Time was up. Dak yanked the Ring from Sera's hand and triggered the warp. But it was already too late.

The scar that cut from Grom's eyebrow to his chin twisted his face as he smiled, letting the arrow fly. It sliced through the air almost in slow motion and it was aimed right at Sera.

"No!" screamed Bill. He launched himself directly into the path of the deadly arrow.

Time and space shimmered around the trio, a sucking sensation gathering in Dak's stomach as it began to pull him out of reality. The last thing he felt was something damp and cold nudging against his free hand.

The last thing he saw was the arrow piercing Bill's chest.

Even as they warped away he could hear Sera's panicked screaming.

21

The Hitchhiker

THE FIRST thing Sera did when she felt solid ground under her feet was throw up. She fell to her knees, oblivious to the damp grass clutched under her fingers as she tried to calm her racing heart and steady her breathing.

Bill. She closed her eyes but she could still see the arrow piercing his chest. The last thing she'd seen of him was his body crumpling, the look on his face one of disbelief. Her stomach heaved again. They had to go back and make sure he was okay.

They *could* go back. The Infinity Ring made it possible.

Something wet brushed her cheek. She turned her head to the side only to be confronted by the smiling maw of a massive beast. It licked her again, its mouth smelling of overripe cabbage.

It whined and nudged her with its nose, almost knocking her over. She wondered if she could somehow still be disoriented from the warp and only imagining things . . . but then realized that her mind would never be able to conjure up a smell as rancid as that dog's breath.

Sera pushed herself to her feet. Her gaze rested on her companions. Riq stood with his arms crossed and one eyebrow raised as if he had a secret he couldn't wait to share.

Dak was completely out of place, his bare chest covered with mud and a wolf pelt wrapped around his shoulders. A wicked-looking axe dangled from one hand while the other rested on the head of the massive beast.

She knew the expression on his face all too well. He'd done something wrong and was hoping she wouldn't notice.

She looked again at the dog and groaned. "Please tell me that creature didn't warp with us from 885 France?"

Dak tried to look contrite. "Her name's Vígi."

Sera pressed a hand to her face as Riq sang, "Someone's in trouble."

"I didn't mean for it to happen!" Dak defended himself. "She nosed my hand when we were warping—there's nothing I could have done."

"Fine," Sera finally managed. "We'll just take her back with us when we go to save Bill." She started programming the Ring.

Riq yanked it from her fingers before she could even input the first coordinate. "Hey!" she cried out, reaching for it, but he held it out of her grasp.

"We're not going back," the older boy said. All traces of his earlier smugness were gone, his expression one of utmost seriousness.

"But you saw what happened," Sera cried. "Bill's hurt—he could be dying."

"Well, technically he's already dead since we warped a millennium ahead," Dak offered.

Sera silenced him with a glare.

Still keeping the Ring out of reach, Riq said, "You said it yourself, Sera, we can't go to the same time and place twice or we could end up triggering the Cataclysm ourselves."

Sera hated having her words flung back in her face. "What I *said* was that every time we warped into a time or a place we caused ripples, but I didn't say they would always turn out catastrophic."

"Where do you draw the line?" Riq argued. "If we can use this thing to go anywhere and any time on a whim, why aren't we going back to 1925 when Pol Pot was born? Why save one guy when we could save six million by stopping Adolf Hitler?"

"We're talking about *Bill,*" she sputtered. "The Hystorian who saved your life!"

Riq's expression didn't waver. "You know I'm right, Sera."

She spun on her heel, stomping a few steps away. She wanted to punch something or scream or both. None of this was fair—Brint and Mari hadn't prepared them for these types of challenges, and she didn't know how to handle them.

She knew Riq was right. But what good was a time-travel device if she couldn't save the people she cared about?

Lingering aftereffects of the Remnant she'd experienced in the church filtered through her mind, twisting around her heart. Sometime, someplace else there had to be other people she cared about, lost to the SQ's quest for power. Tears blurred her vision and she crouched, pressing a hand over her face.

She hated people seeing her cry. Thankfully, the two boys stood behind her, silent and still, probably having no idea what to say or do. But that didn't stop Vígi from padding over to her and leaning her warm body against Sera's side. The massive dog whined, the sound so high-pitched it was almost beyond her hearing. Vígi had also just warped away from someone important to her. They were both sad.

Right then and there, Sera realized just how much she hated the SQ. Before, they'd been more like an opponent — someone she was racing against to save the future. But now, after what the Time Wardens had done to Bill, after what they'd taken away from her, the SQ had become her enemy.

She dug her fingers into the ground, using her new-found anger to ease the aching in her chest. Bill had died to protect her; how many other Hystorians had given their lives for this cause as well? The three of them were part of a legacy now, and they had no other option than to fulfill it to the best of their ability.

As if sensing how uneasy Sera's thoughts had become, Vígi stood and began to pace, stopping every few steps to sniff at the air. Her ears swiveled, listening to the noises of the early morning around them.

Dak snapped his fingers. "I've got it!"

Sera looked up at him with unease. He wore that same expression he got whenever he was about to impart some sort of "imperative" historical fact. She loved how passionate her best friend was about history, but sometimes Sera wished he'd realize that his timing could be a bit off.

"Uh, guys?" Riq asked.

Dak ignored him, excitement brimming in his eyes. "I've been running it through in my head and I knew there was something about Rollo that seemed familiar."

"I think that maybe—" Riq ventured, but Dak cut him off.

"Rollo told me his nickname was Walker, and because of the translation device I didn't hear the word in Old Norse, which would be *Ganger*. I can't believe I didn't put this together earlier, but there's a pretty famous Viking warrior—Ganger Hrolf."

Upon hearing the name, Vígi's tail began to wave furiously through the air. Dak seemed to take that as a good sign as he continued. "At first I thought it was a coincidence, but the thing about Vikings is that their record keeping was terrible—various historians refer to them with different names."

Sera didn't follow what Dak was saying and made a rolling motion with her hand for him to get to the point. "So?"

Beside her, Vígi resumed her pacing, every now and

again stopping to nudge at Dak's hand but he didn't seem to notice.

"Seriously, guys—" Riq ventured again.

Dak looked from Riq to Sera. "Don't you get it?"

They didn't get it. Dak rolled his eyes. "It's the same guy. Rollo is Hrolf, and I've read about Hrolf. I know exactly when and where he's going to be in the summer of 911—we can go back and return Vígi."

"That history was in the old time stream, though," Sera said. "We could have changed it."

Dak shrugged. "It's worth a try, though, isn't it?"

The idea made Sera's pulse pound harder. She might be able to find out what happened to Bill. Just thinking about him caused her chest to tighten. "We really shouldn't be jumping around too much in the time stream, though," she offered halfheartedly, hoping Dak would wave away her concerns. "Even going back for a few minutes could cause ripples."

"Hey!" Riq shouted, stepping between them. Sera finally registered the look of panic on his face. "Whatever we're doing I suggest we do it fast." He pointed over Sera's shoulder and she turned to find a contingent of soldiers running toward them with weapons drawn.

As usual, Dak seemed utterly unconcerned, his mind instead turning to the fascination of a new time period. "What do you think they want?"

Riq rolled his eyes. "I'm guessing they're wondering what a black boy, a savage, a wolf, and a girl wearing a medieval tunic are all doing on the front lawn of the White House."

Old Friends

DAK DIDN'T dare interrupt Sera as her fingers flew over the Infinity Ring, plugging in the date (July 20, 911) and location (the colline de Lèves) he'd given her. He still carried the axe from 885 Paris, but the weapon would be useless against the men bearing down on them. They carried rifles with bayonets on them.

Vígi planted herself in front of Dak, her lips drawn back and body vibrating with a growl. He kept his hand tangled in her ruff, worried that she might bolt after the soldiers. If that happened, they'd never get her back to her master.

Finally Sera cried out, "Got it." She grabbed Riq with one hand, and Riq held on to Dak, and then the world around them began to shimmer and twist. Dak still wasn't used to the way his stomach dropped and his skin seemed to tighten as they warped through time.

It was as if his body knew they were doing something unnatural, and was protesting. It didn't help matters that he had no idea what he'd just gotten them into. According to the history he'd read, the three of them should be warping into the middle of a Viking camp while Rollo celebrated the defeat of the town of Chartres.

Except that he couldn't stop thinking about what Sera had said and it made him uneasy. Of course their involvement in the Siege of Paris had changed history — that was the point of going back to fix the Breaks.

What if the Battle of Chartres never happened? What if Rollo wasn't there? Realizing that the history he knew and understood so intimately no longer existed was more disorienting than the feeling of being whipped through time.

These thoughts still whirled through Dak's mind as everything around him grew still. They stood on the slope of a hill in the darkness, only a sliver of moon and wash of stars overhead to light their surroundings.

Sera let out a long breath. "This looks right," she whispered.

Dak heard the soft murmur of voices from somewhere up the hill and felt Vígi tense under his fingers. She raised her head, sniffing at the air. Curious, Dak sniffed, too. He smelled woodsmoke and copper, dirt and sweat.

Before he could get a better grip on the dog, she bolted. Dak didn't think twice before chasing after her. As he ran he heard Sera and Riq following, crashing through the underbrush.

The dog slowed at the edge of a clearing, her steps silent in the night, and Dak did his best to quiet his own steps. But Sera and Riq weren't as stealthy as they tried to catch up, and it was no surprise when a cluster of burly Viking warriors intercepted them and began asking questions.

Instinctively, Dak felt his fingers tighten around his own axe to defend himself and his friends — then he realized that the Vikings didn't seem to be paying him any attention. Only belatedly did he remember he was still dressed as a *berserkr* from the battle in Paris; he was actually blending in.

Vígi paused and whined, and for a moment Dak felt torn between his friends and the dog. His mind was made up when Vígi pressed her nose against the back of Dak's knee, urging him forward. "They're with me," he called over his shoulder as he continued running.

The center of the camp was subdued — nothing like Dak would have expected after such a huge victory as the Battle of Chartres had been. A knot of unease began to tighten in his stomach.

A giant of a Viking sat in front of the remains of a fire, the glowing embers casting shadows on his face. His shoulders were slumped, his empty hands hanging limp and his hair graying to white. Dak knew it must be Rollo — who else could be so massive? — but this man bore little resemblance to the laughing, high-spirited warrior Dak knew.

Whatever the three of them had done to change history hadn't been kind to Rollo, Dak realized.

He slowed his approach, but Vígi showed no such hesitation. She raced across the clearing, tongue lolling from her mouth, and then leapt through the air, landing fully against the Viking's chest and pushing him from his stool.

The man fell to the ground with a crash, the dog crouched over him. She tilted her head back and let loose with a happy howl before lapping at his face.

"Ugh, ick!" he grumbled, and Dak smiled at the reversal.

The giant pushed to his elbows, no easy feat with a one-hundred-fifty-plus pound dog perched on one's chest. "Vígi?" he whispered, his voice almost cracking. Dak wasn't sure, but he thought the warrior's eyes might have been glistening.

The beast's tail thumped heartily, her face breaking into a grin that bared every single gleaming tooth. She licked at the Viking again. "Only one dog I know with breath as vile as that," he muttered, scratching at the dog's ears. "But how?"

His gaze snapped up, landing on Dak. Rollo's face lit up. "My time-traveling friend!" he said, rising to his feet. He pulled Dak into a hug that felt like it might have cracked several ribs.

"Come! Join me at the fire and tell me of your travels," Rollo boomed. He motioned over Dak's head, and Dak turned to find Sera and Riq being escorted into camp. They seemed to visibly relax when they saw Vígi sitting happily by Rollo's side.

"We just needed to run this one errand and really don't have time to sit and chat—" Dak started to say.

Rollo roared with laughter. "With your shiny Ring, all you have is time."

While Riq and Dak chuckled, Sera stepped forward, her face grim and serious. She twisted her hands together in front of her anxiously. "I know it was a long time ago for you," she said. "But when we warped away a boy by the name of Billfrith was there in the church and he was hurt. Do you know what happened to him?"

Rollo's eyebrows drew together, his expression one of curiosity. He cupped one hand around his mouth and shouted, "Bill!" before turning back to Sera and saying, "Why don't you let him tell you?"

The Horns of War (Again)

SERA WAS pretty sure her heart stopped beating. Her hands tightened until her nails dug into her palms. The echo of Rollo shouting Bill's name resounded in her ears.

There's no way, she thought as her pulse stuttered and began to gallop.

From behind her she heard someone whisper, "Sera?" The voice was just as she remembered it, causing her cheeks to heat and a smile to break across her face.

He was not only alive but she got to see him again! It was beyond her wildest dreams!

She was already calling out his name as she spun on her heel and came face-to-face with a man who looked to be as old as her uncle. His hair thinned around his temples, and wrinkles crowded the corners of his eyes.

She choked on his name. Of course he was older, her mind tried to reason. While she'd just left him no more than twenty minutes ago, he'd lived an entire life apart from her.

She heard herself cry out as her eyes blurred with tears.

Bill reached out a hand toward her, tentatively, but it was the way a father might move to comfort a child.

Sera turned and fled.

She didn't get far into the woods before reason pulled her up short. It was dark, and she was near a battlefield. It was stupid of her to continue running. She pressed her back against a tree and sank to the ground. Blindly, she stared at her hands in her lap.

Less than an hour ago Bill had twined his fingers through hers. He'd leaned toward her and she'd thought she might be about to experience her first kiss. Her stomach twisted as her brain warred between the two time lines, trying to orient her.

She heard Bill coming even before he called out her name, softly. She closed her eyes—his voice really was exactly the same as she remembered. For a moment she was convinced he'd appear as he'd been before.

But when she opened her eyes he stood there, still so much older. He sat down next to her.

"This is strange, isn't it?" he asked.

She could only nod.

"I thought about you after . . ." He took a deep breath and ran his hand through his graying hair, such a familiar gesture. "In my mind you were growing older, just like I was. Seeing you now, exactly how you were when you left . . ." He trailed off.

Sera forced a swallow. She couldn't bring herself to meet his eyes. "What happened? The last I saw you'd been hit by an arrow."

"I got lucky. It was a clean wound—didn't hit

anything important." He eased the collar of his tunic aside and in the soft glow of the night Sera saw a puckered scar. "Rollo was able to fend off the rest of Siegfried's men. He waited until dark to take me back to the camp and dress the wound. That's when we put two and two together and realized that his great-grandfather is the one who saved my great-great-great-uncle. Once we realized all we had in common, I joined up with him.

"I thought Siegfried would be angry after Rollo let you guys escape, but once Rollo told him that there was a lot of land worth plundering down the Seine in Burgundy and that he'd let Siegfried have it all, that seemed to smooth things over. Then they went their separate ways — Siegfried and his men carrying their ships overland to farther down the river, and Rollo staying behind outside Paris for a while until King Charles the Fat finally paid him to leave."

He picked up a stick from the ground and began to break it into smaller segments. "It feels like it was ages ago." After a pause he asked, "How has it been saving the future?"

Sera still didn't lift her eyes. "We haven't been. When we realized Vígi had hitched a ride we came back here to return her. I . . ." She swallowed with effort. "I thought you'd been killed trying to save my life."

He reached out and lifted her chin with a finger. "If I had died for you, it would have been worth it. The cause of the Hystorians means everything to me."

She realized, then, that's what she'd been to him. Not

a girl he liked, but a part of a larger cause that needed protecting. She stood abruptly. "I need to get back to the others. We shouldn't even have come to this time—it's dangerous to interfere."

"Wait." He stood, but age had made him slower and she was already several steps away. "There's something you should know."

Her shoulders tensed. She just wanted to leave, for this whole night to end. She wanted to remember Bill as he'd been before, not this stranger.

"You told me that in order to fix the Break the Vikings had to be kept away from Normandy, right?" he asked.

Sera nodded without turning to face him. "If Siegfried went to Burgundy instead, then we did our job."

"Siegfried recently changed his mind," Bill said. "That's why we're here. Rollo's trying to fight his way into Normandy by way of Chartres. But he lost the battle today—"

Sera spun toward him. "Dak said Rollo won Chartres. That's why we came here."

Bill shook his head. "We lost today, Sera. And this was Rollo's last chance to get ahead of Siegfried."

"We have a problem," Dak said as soon as he saw Sera striding back into camp. She didn't look happy to see him, but that had never stopped Dak before.

"If this is about cheese, so help me . . ."

"Rollo lost the battle today," he said, keeping his

voice low. Dak still couldn't get over the changes in his Viking friend's appearance. Where before he'd strode through camp with his wide shoulders thrown back and chin high, now he slumped forward on his stool, staring at the fire. Every now and again Vígi would nudge his hand with her nose and he'd smile down at her, but Dak knew that his defeat earlier today had been a crushing blow.

And it shouldn't have happened. It wouldn't have if Dak, Sera, and Riq hadn't been mucking around in history. By getting Rollo involved, they'd practically ruined his life.

Dak glanced around the clearing and lowered his voice even more. "Rollo said the Franks have surrounded the hill. They've completely cut him off from water . . . and his ships. If they attack, he has no hope of fending them off."

Riq strolled over just in time to hear this last bit. "Then I'd say now would be a fine time for us to fire up the Infinity Ring and catch the first warp out of here."

"We can't," Sera said simply. For once Dak and Riq were on the same page as they both stared at her with confusion.

"Come again?" Riq asked, taking the words right out of Dak's mouth.

Dak noticed Sera glancing over her shoulder to where Bill hovered around the edges of camp. "It's worse than you realize," she whispered.

"Worse than being sitting ducks for an army three times our size?" Dak asked.

She leveled her gaze at him and Dak's stomach sank. He knew that expression. It was the same one she'd worn just before their fourth-grade science fair when she'd found out she wasn't the only student who'd thought of using demotic technology to monitor household energy use.

"Siegfried's marching on Normandy and there are other SQ Vikings behind him ready to take his place if he falls," she said. "Rollo was headed there to try to stop them. But the Franks have this hill surrounded, and if he can't find a way out, he won't be able to confront Siegfried. And we'll have failed to fix the Break."

24

Old Enemies

IF THERE'S one thing that always calmed Sera it was losing herself in the intricacies of physics. The world could be falling apart outside (and with all the earthquakes, tornadoes, and hurricanes roaring about it in the twenty-first century, it sometimes was) and she'd never notice. She'd always had the ability to focus in on problems with a laser-like precision and she hated nothing more than failing to come up with a proper solution.

After all, she was the girl who'd stayed up for two days straight figuring out the previously unsolvable Yang–Mills existence and mass gap problem.

But now she didn't have two days to figure out a solution to their situation; she was lucky if she had two hours before dawn came and the Franks attacked. Rollo and his men had been arguing much of the night, Dak interjecting at times, trying to figure out how a few thousand Viking warriors could fight their way past tens of thousands of Frankish and Burgundian soldiers.

They'd all come to the same conclusion: It wasn't

possible. Every avenue of retreat had been cut off by the Franks. Even though the fleet of Viking ships floated less than a league away, it might as well have been the distance to the moon.

Yet a feeling in Sera's stomach told her she was missing something obvious. She stood from the fire and walked slowly through camp. Everything was so quiet and subdued, nothing like their previous battle experience, full of urgency and hasty preparations.

A part of her missed the noise. Even though it had been terrifying at the time, there had been something thrilling about the clanging Parisian church bells and the blaring Viking horns signaling the start of battle.

Sera froze, one foot still suspended in the air. "That's it," she said out loud to no one. She laughed at how perfect of a solution it was as she raced back to Dak and Rollo.

She was winded when she found them in front of the fire. "The horns," she blurted excitedly. "We may not have enough men to fight the Franks, but they don't have to know that. Dak, Riq, and I will sneak into their camps with battle horns and start sounding them—the Franks will assume they're under attack and scatter. In the confusion, you run for the ships!"

She beamed with pride.

Rollo scowled. "I'm not sending kids into the enemy camp," he grumbled.

Dak bristled at being called a kid, but before he could complain Sera piped up.

"No one would ever suspect the three of us," she argued. "If the Franks find a Viking wandering in the woods they'll get suspicious and everything will be ruined. But if it's just us . . ." She shrugged. "We're kids, how much trouble could we be?"

Dak was glad that before leaving the Viking camp he'd finally been able to change out of his wolf pelt, replacing it with dark leggings and a thick cloak pulled from an injured Frankish soldier. His familiar axe still rested at his hip, and in his hands he carried a large war horn.

Clouds had rolled in while they'd debated the details of Sera's plan. Now, even though dawn was imminent, the night was pitch-black, which made navigation rather difficult. Dak had never been a particularly graceful individual and not being able to see where he was going wasn't helping matters. Every step he took seemed to bring with it a cacophony of cracking branches that caused him to jump (which only set off more noises).

After finally agreeing to the plan (it took a lot of arguing), Rollo warned the three time travelers not to get too near to the Frankish camps. They'd likely have guards posted, he warned, and they couldn't risk getting caught.

At first Dak obeyed this command but the longer he waited out past the edge of the camps, the more restless he became. After all, he was a historian first and foremost, and he saw it as his duty to properly record what he witnessed throughout time. He'd already begun drafting his magnum opus, titled *The Time Lord*, which, he was quite sure, would establish him as the preeminent authority on all things historical.

Besides, it was boring out in the woods alone. His mind made up (not that he took much convincing), Dak moved toward the Frankish camp. The closer he got without anyone sounding an alarm, the bolder he grew.

He kept himself tucked low as he advanced through a collection of lean-tos, pausing every now and again to listen to the snores of the soldiers. His heart pounded with a mixture of fear and excitement.

Dak was just peeking his head into a crudely built cabin when he heard the first horn blow: Sera. The sound sputtered at first and then gained in volume and urgency. Another horn joined in: Riq.

Already the sound of mumbling and surprise drifted among the soldiers scattered throughout the tents and bedrolls littered around the camp. A few men popped to their feet, weapons already drawn.

There was no time for Dak to sneak back out to the thick woods and so he did the only thing he could: hunkered down behind the nearest tree and blew his horn as hard and loud as possible.

It looked easier than it was. At first the instrument only let out a wheezing, choking sound. Dak's cheeks began to blaze hot and red with the effort, his head spinning with light-headedness as he heaved in another breath. He changed the shape of his mouth and that did the trick: The horn let out a horrid, piercing wail.

Whoever hadn't been woken by the other horns was certainly awake now. Soldiers sprang from their bedrolls, some of them yanking on shoes, some of them reaching for weapons, but most merely fleeing.

"The North Men are attacking!" Dak yelled, encouraging their panic. "Retreat!" His warning spread like wildfire, and Dak heard it repeated again and again. Soldiers scrambled, fleeing the camp so fast that Dak couldn't help laughing in between bouts of blowing the war horn.

The ruse had worked; the Frankish army was in disarray, which is exactly what the Vikings needed to break toward the river. He couldn't wait to meet up with Sera and congratulate her on such a brilliant plan. Especially since he'd never really been convinced it would work in the first place.

With a smile on his face, Dak turned toward the cover of the forest—when a hand suddenly clamped on his shoulder. Dak reached for his axe, but he was disarmed immediately and found himself pinned to the ground, staring up at the dawn-tinged sky.

A figure hovered over him, sharp knee digging against Dak's ribs. "If it isn't my old nemesis," the man said. "You don't seem to have aged a day."

He hauled Dak to his feet and dragged him toward a fire. As the light spilled over the man's face, illuminating the scar that slashed from his left eyebrow to the right corner of his mouth, Dak felt his insides twist.

Even though the past twenty-five years had added wrinkles and age spots to the soldier's face, Dak recognized Gorm instantly. The aged man yanked Dak's hands behind his back, tying them tightly with a length of rope he'd been using as a belt.

"You don't have to do that," Dak muttered.

The Time Warden barked out a laugh. "That's what the man and woman said, too. And since they were older I believed them. That's the last time I trust anyone from the future."

Dak's heart froze. He swallowed. "A man and woman? From the future?" It could only be his parents.

"Head still hurts from where the woman conked me with a rock," Gorm grumbled. Then he gave Dak an evil look. "I'm not taking any chances this time."

25

Inheritance

SUDDENLY, NOTHING mattered more to Dak than getting back to Sera and Riq. And if that meant leading the Time Warden right to where Rollo and his men were clambering into their ships, so be it.

He had to tell Sera about his parents. If the knot on Gorm's head was as fresh as it looked, they'd been here only an hour or two ago. They could *still* be here, somewhere. It took everything Dak had not to start calling out for them in the dusky dawn.

If the Time Warden was suspicious that Dak offered only a halfhearted resistance before giving in to his demands to be taken to the Vikings, he didn't show it. Instead he just trudged along behind Dak, recounting how losing the time travelers in 885 had caused Siegfried to banish him and how miserable his life with the Frankish army had been ever since.

Dak didn't care and he barely listened.

"Siegfried took my sword, *Leggbítr*," Gorm grumbled. "Do you know what it's like for a Norseman to have his weapon taken from him?"

When Dak didn't answer Gorm prodded him in the back to elicit the correct response. Dak shook his head.

"Humiliating. *Leggbítr* was my father's sword and his father's before him. And what do I have to pass on to my own son?"

Dak glanced back at the Time Warden, wondering if his son had inherited his thick nose and drooping ears. If so, he should be glad to get nothing else from his father.

Another shove to the back and Dak mumbled, "What?" He tried not to think about what Sera and Riq would say when he led the enemy into their midst. He was being stupid and he knew it and yet he didn't turn back.

"Nothing," Gorm barked. "That is, until I trade that magical metal device to Siegfried. You take me to camp, you give me the thingy, and maybe I let you live. Deal?"

As if to emphasize his point, Gorm swung his axe through the air, cleanly slicing a thick limb from a nearby tree. His message was clear: If things didn't go well, that could be Dak's neck. He shivered, trying to shake off Gorm's all-too-real threat.

When Sera realized what Dak was doing she was going to be so ticked off. But that didn't matter to Dak right now. What mattered was figuring out how to find his parents again.

"He should be here by now," Sera hissed. She walked in tight circles along the shore of the misty Eure River while Riq sat along the bank skipping rocks across the water. It was a cloud-choked morning and the stones sailed into the gray before sinking.

"It's Dak," Riq answered. "I'd be surprised to see him again before noon."

Sera whirled on him, crossing her arms over her chest. "What's that supposed to mean?"

One of Riq's rocks sank into the water with a loud *sploosh*. He lifted a shoulder. "Only that it's Dak. We let him go alone to an enemy camp. I figured we had a fifty-fifty chance he wouldn't do something stupid and get caught."

Sera felt her blood boil hot in indignation and then drain from her cheeks in worry. "Dak's smarter than that. I'm sure he learned his lesson last time," she said.

"When hasn't he gotten in trouble? Alone *or* with us? Look, I understand the dude's fascination with history — this whole trip must be like a field day to him. But he's not exactly smart about avoiding risks and taking precautions."

Sera wanted to argue. She even opened her mouth, ready to defend Dak. But nothing came out. The truth was, Riq was right.

With a huff, Sera turned her back and resumed her pacing. Just downriver Rollo and his men were piling supplies into their tethered boats and preparing to cast off. With so many men, it would be a long and involved process but if Sera, Riq, and Dak wanted to be with them when they left, they had to be ready soon.

It wouldn't be long before the Franks realized that the Viking attack had been nothing but a ruse and then they'd regroup and come after them. She really didn't want to stick around to see what an enraged Frank looked like in this century.

For a while longer, Sera began to pace and then she stopped in front of Riq. Losing Dak wasn't the only problem occupying her mind.

"Do you think getting Rollo out of here is enough to fix the Break?" she asked.

Riq just shook his head.

"And you're basing that on . . . ?"

Riq looked up at her and she glimpsed something familiar in his eyes. "My Remnants are getting worse," he confessed.

Sera winced. "That bad?"

Riq tried to laugh but the sound came out forced and choked. Sera sat next to him, watching his face closely.

"You never told me what your Remnants were about," she said.

Riq scratched at the ground, searching for another rock. "There's nothing to really say about them. Nothing concrete I can describe."

"Mine were like that, too, at first," Sera said. "They were just feelings but eventually I started to understand what those feelings meant." She hesitated before prodding. "What's the feeling you get from yours?"

Riq pushed himself to his feet and stretched, throwing his arms high overhead. "Nothing," he said when he was done.

Sera hated the attitude in his voice. "Fine, if you don't want to share then don't." She stood and walked away. "I'm going after Dak," she said.

Caught

DAK GRITTED his teeth in frustration. He didn't care so much that his hands were tied behind his back, or that the Time Warden now carried Dak's axe, or even that his parents might be nearby but he didn't know where.

All of those things he could deal with. What angered him was that he'd just heard a familiar voice call his name. Sera had never been one for subtlety and she crashed around in the forest sounding like his uncle Dick after eating Aunt Lou's world-famous six-bean casserole.

Dak tried to cough every time he heard her voice to distract the Time Warden but that only served to make Gorm send strange looks his way. Dak could hear the edge of panic in Sera's voice. It was careless of her to be wandering around in the woods looking for him. There was a Frankish army on the run, what if she stumbled on them instead?

Eventually, Gorm figured it out. He jerked on Dak's arms, pulling him to a stop. "Sounds like your friend's worried about you," he said, nudging Dak with his elbow.

Dak fumed but when the Time Warden raised the axe to Dak's neck and ordered him to call out for Sera, he had no choice but to obey. "Sera Froste!" he shouted, hoping that by using her full name she'd be suspicious and figure something was up.

They really should have figured out some sort of code word for situations like this. Though perhaps it would be better to try avoiding situations like this altogether.

Sera was one of the smartest people Dak knew—other than himself, of course—but she was more of what he'd call book smart rather than street smart (or in this case, forest smart). So he shouldn't have been surprised when she came crashing through the underbrush, winded and unarmed.

The Time Warden was delighted to see her. "Well, now it's getting interesting, isn't it?"

She drew up short, her eyes going wide as she glanced from Gorm to the axe to Dak with his hands tied behind his back. All she said was, "Uh-oh."

Uh-oh, indeed, Dak thought. Now all they needed was for Riq to join them and it could be a party.

As if summoned by Dak's thoughts, the older boy stumbled into the clearing, just as unarmed as Sera.

"Oh, for the love of mincemeat," Dak muttered, using Sera's favorite phrase. She glared at him.

"You didn't bring any weapons, or perhaps a Viking or twenty as backup, did you?" Dak asked hopefully.

At least Sera had the decency to look sheepish as she shrugged and said, "All the men were busy."

Great, Dak thought. Now Gorm knew no one was coming to rescue them. This morning was getting worse and worse.

Which of course is a phrase only uttered moments before things do indeed become worse. Gorm knocked Dak to the ground and stepped forward, resting the axe against Sera's stomach. Using delicacy that Dak never could have thought possible with such an unwieldy weapon, the Time Warden sliced the leather sack from her belt.

The Infinity Ring had been their last bargaining chip. Now that it was in the Time Warden's possession, the three time travelers were completely out of options.

For a moment Sera wondered if perhaps her luck had run out. She'd already come up with one successful ruse tonight and she wasn't confident she'd be able to pull off another. She was pretty sure that fear showed on her face, which is part of why it was so easy to convince the Time Warden that she and Riq were the only people in the woods coming after Dak.

Also, technically, that was a true statement. Not that Sera was one for lying, but she was very much a stickler for details and precision. Dak had asked her if there were any Viking men assisting them with backup and she was quite confident in answering no.

But that didn't mean she didn't have other tricks up her sleeve. She hoped.

Even so, feeling the sharp edge of the Time Warden's blade against her and watching as he plucked the Infinity Ring away was quite worrying.

What if she'd miscalculated? If the next few moments went wrong, the three of them could lose all ties to the future, fail in their quest to fix the Breaks, and even possibly lose their lives.

The Time Warden pulled the Infinity Ring from its bag and sniffed it before putting it between his teeth and biting. Pretty much everyone in the clearing winced at the sound of a tooth cracking.

"Hydroxylapatite-infused bone really isn't much of a match against titanium," Sera cautioned.

The Time Warden glared at her and raised his axe. She took a hasty step back but wasn't fast enough — Gorm grabbed her by the arm.

Her gaze shifted to Dak and what she saw there made her remaining confidence waver. He was well and truly terrified and, with his arms tied behind his back, there was nothing he could do to defend himself. Or her.

Riq tried to step forward and situate himself between Sera and the Time Warden but that only made the older man angrier and caused him to push the blade against her throat. With every swallow she felt the keen edge of it, and her mind couldn't stop cycling through just how much force and pressure it would take for him to sever something important.

He was nervous, that much was clear, and Sera knew well enough that a man on edge was liable to take desperate measures. Especially since he had the Infinity Ring in his grasp.

Something shifted in the woods to her left, a dark shape creeping through the darkness. Seeing it, Sera's heart began to pound wildly. This was her chance, the moment she'd planned for. She had to take action and she had to do it now. She closed her eyes, took a deep breath, and crossed her fingers, hoping that her luck hadn't run out after all.

If she failed, it wasn't just their lives at stake, but the fate of the world.

27

Admitting Defeat

"Vígi," Sera shouted. She pointed her finger at the Time Warden and added the command, "Dinner!" For a moment nothing happened and Sera's breath hitched as her lungs felt impossibly tight.

Growing up, Sera's uncle had never allowed her to have a pet and so she'd always looked at dogs and cats with a certain amount of puzzlement. She didn't understand why someone would invite a wild creature into their home and attempt to interact with it on a daily basis.

But over the past day she'd begun to understand the bond between a dog and its master, especially after seeing how desperate and depressed Vígi became when she was separated from Rollo.

Not to mention the way the Viking chieftain's eyes lit up when he saw his beloved beast again. It was like watching a father reunite with a long-lost child.

At this moment in time, though, as Vígi propelled herself into the clearing, Sera could have kissed that dog, horrid breath notwithstanding.

The Time Warden didn't even have a chance to prepare himself before the massive beast leapt through the air, tackling him to the ground and placing her mouth around his throat.

He froze as Vígi's teeth pressed gently against his skin. Sera noticed Dak wince—he'd already told the story of being pinned by Vígi the first time he met her and how terrifying the experience had been.

"You hungry, girl?" Sera asked, enjoying the look of panic on Gorm's face. She wasn't sure which was worse for the man: the dog's teeth at his throat or her breath so close to his nose.

She ran her hand along the dog's bristled back in thanks as she bent to snatch the axe from the Time Warden's hands. It didn't take long to slice through the ropes binding Dak's hands behind his back.

Newly freed, Dak knelt to give Vígi a good scratching behind her ears. The dog's tail swung happily through the air in response.

"Are you going to behave?" Sera asked, looming over the fallen Viking. "Or shall I let this fine dog enjoy her meal?"

The man's face burned red. "I'm not the only one, you know," he hissed. "Kill me if you want, but there are others like me after you and none of them have a reason to see you kept alive. You don't even know what mistake you've made here today."

Sera started to answer when Dak leaned in close, all playfulness draining from his face. "Where are my parents? The couple you saw earlier—where did they go?"

It was such an unexpected question that Sera gasped.

Apparently, her reaction was all the Time Warden needed. A slow grin broke across his face. In response Vígi's jaws tightened ever so slightly, making the man wince.

Sera glanced at Dak, urging him to look up at her. Usually they had the ability to almost read each other's thoughts. There were times they were so in sync it's like they shared the same brain (albeit his tended to focus on more esoteric historical details while hers was firmly rooted in scientific fact).

Now, they were almost like strangers. Sera couldn't begin to guess what was going through Dak's mind. The expression on his face, a mix of despair and rage, was one she'd never seen before.

Gorm chuckled. "So it seems there might be something the young time traveler wants after all." Even with his life at stake, the Time Warden managed to lift one eyebrow. "What are you willing to trade for that information?"

In the distance she heard men calling out orders, the Frankish army regrouping and setting off toward the Viking encampment along the river. They were running out of time.

"Dak," she said, plucking at the edge of his cloak. "We have to go."

When he looked up at her, his face was twisted in desperation. "It's my parents, Sera. I know you don't understand but . . ."

He must have seen the way his words dug into her heart because he trailed off. Riq cleared his throat then, making his presence known. He knew enough about Sera's Remnants to realize how much Dak's words stung.

She *did* understand what it was like to miss your parents. Every time her stomach twisted and the world tilted into a Remnant, that's what she felt. She was always aware of the gap in her life left by her parents' deaths.

"Let's go," Riq murmured. Sera knew he was right. The Franks were drawing closer and if the Time Warden was telling the truth, more SQ cronies were embedded in the army coming after them.

She tugged harder at Dak. He hesitated and then she felt him give in. Vígi stood her ground, keeping the Time Warden pinned so they could get away without being followed. As the three time travelers ran into the woods the man shouted, "You can't escape the SQ. Through time and space — we'll always be a step ahead!"

The three of them didn't say much as they fled upriver toward the fleet of Viking ships, which suited Dak just fine. He'd been impressed by Sera's quick thinking — even he'd been duped by her ruse — but that couldn't take his mind off his parents.

They'd made it to the band of Vikings and were being escorted onto one of the ships when Dak stopped short, holding Sera and Riq back. "What if Gorm actually knows where my parents are? We might be leaving the only real lead we have to finding them."

Men bustled around them, loading up the ships and

setting their shields along the strakes for protection. The first light of morning was still struggling just above the horizon and a soft mist curled up from the surface of the river. Rollo's ship had already pushed from the bank and unfurled its sail, the crisp dawn air making the bright red cloth flutter. He let out a sharp whistle, calling for his dog.

"The fact that he saw your parents only confirms our theory about the Breaks," Sera said, out of breath from running. He could tell she was trying to be patient with him, though an edge still crept into her voice. "They're drawn to the Breaks. If we don't find them here and now, we'll have another chance. I just know it."

Dak wanted to believe her but . . . "But this wasn't supposed to be a Break," he told her. "We went back to 885 to fix it—we were never supposed to be here. In fact, we *wouldn't* be here if it weren't for Vigi."

Instead of responding, Sera strode toward one of the ships and let a burly Viking boost her on board.

"Wait," Dak called after her. The boat was packed with people and supplies, and Dak had to thread his way through large men preparing to cast off. When he finally caught up with Sera in the bow she wouldn't meet his eye. "What aren't you telling me?" he asked.

"I think the Hystorians sent us to the wrong time in the first place," she answered softly. "I don't think we were ever meant to be at the Siege of Paris after all."

2 8

Learning from Dogs

DAK COULD tell how much Sera disliked admitting that they might have made a mistake and apparently Riq felt the same. He scowled. "I decoded that clue correctly," he told them. "I may be younger than Brint and Mari, but I understand The Art of Memory and how to use it. It's just like any other language," he grumbled.

Sera sighed. "I'm not saying you were wrong, it's just . . ." She ran a hand through her hair and seemed surprised to find it so short. She frowned and Dak remembered how much she'd loved her long hair. Her uncle had once told her it made her look like her mother.

He hadn't realized just how much she was sacrificing when she allowed Gloria the Hystorian to cut it off during their first mission.

The ship pulled away from shore, men bent over the oars to push them against the current. The movement jolted Dak and he grabbed for the nearest bench to steady himself. Already he could hear the sound of the approaching Frankish soldiers and see shadows of armed men running through the trees along the riverbank.

"I think that Brint and Mari might have gotten it wrong," Sera told him. "Which means we can't rely on the SQuare nearly as much as we have been."

Dak felt entirely too exposed and vulnerable, even though the river around them was filled with ships, each one teeming with Vikings aiming bows and arrows toward the shore. "We really don't know what we're doing, do we?"

Sera cringed at the question. He knew Sera hated when she didn't know something, and it was even worse when someone pointed it out, especially a friend.

Riq stepped forward, his hands fisted. "We're doing the best we can," he said. "Sera's saved your butt more times than I can count—even when you didn't realize it. We were under a lot of pressure to warp away when you were out gallivanting with the Vikings. But we didn't."

Dak tried to catch Sera's eyes, wondering if this was true, but she avoided his gaze.

"Whatever," he eventually mumbled. "Let's just get to the next Break and start looking for my parents again. Is the Ring already programmed?"

Sera and Riq traded a glance, something Dak was getting really tired of. He hated feeling out of the loop.

She took a deep breath. "There's a problem with that," she started. "My Remnants have been getting worse. Riq and I both think it means we haven't fixed anything yet."

"But we kept Siegfried from controlling Normandy," Dak argued. "Now his descendants won't conquer Great

Britain and establish dominance throughout Europe. Isn't that what we were supposed to do?"

"We just delayed the inevitable. Now Siegfried is going to Normandy by way of Burgundy instead of Paris. The result is the same." Sera began to pace. It's what she always did when she was frustrated that a solution to a problem was escaping her.

"The SQ knew what they were doing when they aligned with the Vikings," Riq added. "They're crazy good warriors. If they want Normandy, they're going to take it. Even if Rollo gets there first, they'll just end up fighting him for it. And since our Remnants haven't gotten any better, it's a pretty good bet Seigfried and his men will win. We had our chance to fix things before and we blew it. As far as I can tell, there's nothing we can do to stop the SQ now."

Giving up was not a phrase in Sera's vocabulary. But her scientific mind required that she base her actions on facts and those were starting to add up against her.

Everything should have led Sera to the conclusion that they'd failed. But she just couldn't believe that. She'd identified a tenth dimension in string theory because she'd been unwilling to give up and she wasn't about to start doing that now.

That still didn't mean she had any solutions to their current predicament.

She saw Bill pushing his way through the men on

the ship, finding his way to her. Her stomach twisted every time she looked at him, trying to reconcile the Bill she knew before with who he was now. He was an old man and she couldn't figure out how to relate to him. The day before he'd been a friend and confidant. Now . . . she didn't know what he was now.

She turned away and looked out over the water so that she didn't have to meet his eyes.

"We have word that King Charles the Simple's army is marshaling troops upriver and the Franks are regrouping behind us," he told them. "They'll both be striking out for us soon. It won't be safe here much longer. Rollo intends to fight, but even if we're successful I'm afraid we don't have much hope of stopping Siegfried's forces. You may want to move on before things get messy."

"Yeah," Riq quipped. "Because warping into yet another war zone is so appealing."

Dak seemed to ignore him, as usual. "What's the king doing in this part of France?" Sera rolled her eyes. Leave it to her best friend to turn any moment into a quest for more historical knowledge.

"Oh, he's been trying to draft some sort of treaty between the Norsemen and the Franks to keep them from constantly fighting but so far he's been unsuccessful. . . ."

Bill continued his history lesson, Dak hanging on every word, but Sera was distracted by the sight of Vígi loping up the riverbank alongside them, licking her chops as if she'd just enjoyed a fine meal.

Rollo's boat was at the head of the mass of ships, its sail full and oars slicing through the water. From the helm the giant Viking chieftain let out another piercing whistle that caused the dog's ears to perk and flick in his direction.

Vígi's muscles bunched and she raced toward the river, claws digging through the mud. She didn't even hesitate at the water's edge, just dove in with a splash and began to paddle furiously, the tip of her tail weaving through the water behind her.

Rollo laughed and called out encouragement as Vígi drew closer. When she reached the edge of his ship he leaned over and plucked her from the water, not caring that he almost capsized the boat in the process.

Even from where she was standing Sera could hear the way Rollo crooned to Vígi, letting her sopping body settle in his massive lap as she licked at his face happily. Every time her tail swung it sent out an arc of water, drenching the men stationed at the oars, but neither dog nor master noticed or cared.

Sera couldn't help but smile. Even though they'd risked screwing up the time line by warping here to return Vígi to her master, it was worth it to see how happy she made the Viking chieftain. And he deserved to have his dog back after he'd done so much to help the three time travelers.

As soon as that thought crossed her mind, Sera gasped. Of course! The solution was so obvious that she started to laugh hard enough for tears to leak down her cheeks.

When she caught her breath she realized that Dak, Riq, and Bill were all staring at her with concern. She suppressed a few more chuckles and cleared her throat before announcing, "We've been looking at this the wrong way. I figured out how to fix the Break."

They continued to stare at her, eyes wide with expectation.

She turned to Bill. They'd need his expertise to make it work. "How quickly can you get us to the king?"

29

So Close, So Far Away

SERA COULDN'T stop beaming. They'd been looking at the problem all wrong. Riq had been right, there was nothing the three of them could do to keep the Vikings from occupying Normandy. So the solution was obvious: They had to pick the *right* Viking to take charge. And Rollo was the perfect candidate.

It was brilliant in its simplicity. And best of all, it involved making peace instead of war.

Even though it had been her idea to approach King Charles the Simple with the idea of granting Rollo the land that would one day become Normandy in exchange for his promise to protect the mouth of the Seine from further Viking attacks, it had been Bill who'd pulled it all off. They'd known there was no way the king would listen to three kids, and Bill knew that the fate of the world rested on his ability to get this deal done.

He'd been hesitant to accept the task at first. He explained he'd always seen his role as Hystorian as being to keep records and support the time travelers, not to take such an active role. But as a native Parisian who had spent decades among the Vikings, he was the perfect ambassador. It had taken the entire boat trip up the river to the king's camp to convince him, but in the end Sera was the one to get him to agree.

After that it had been a long and tense ride. The boats were crowded and Sera spent the entire time anxious about the impending meeting. She knew her plan was a long shot — why would the king even accept an audience with them, much less agree to their proposal? After all, according to Dak, Charles the Simple ruled over the Franks — he owned the river they were traveling on, the land along the banks, and everything she could see.

At the same time, she saw no other way to fix the Break. They had to secure Normandy and the lineage that would rule it. She trusted Rollo and she trusted Bill to convince the king of what they needed.

Once they arrived at the edge of the king's camp, they spent several tense hours waiting to find out if they could even speak with anyone who might listen to their ideas. They could all just as easily been taken prisoner. Sera tried not to squeal with glee when a dour-looking set of soldiers led their small group to a large, ornate tent with smoke drifting from a peak at the top.

"It's the king's tent," Dak whispered out of the corner of his mouth as the flaps were pulled aside and the soldier motioned for them to enter.

That was pretty much the point at which Sera's mind went blank. She knew she'd stood before the king, and she remembered being proud of the way Bill's voice didn't tremble even when her hands shook so hard she had to grasp them behind her back.

At first the king balked at the idea of ceding away so much land to a Norseman, but Bill explained that Rollo would swear fealty, making himself a subject of the king and bound by his laws — something Vikings rarely ever did — and promise to guard against future Viking invasions by stopping them from entering the Seine.

The king was tired of Viking invasions, which made it that much easier for Bill to persuade him to sign off on the deal.

They'd thought that convincing Rollo would be another matter entirely but when they approached him with the solution he merely shrugged. "I was getting too old for plundering anyway," he'd told them. "Besides, now that I've got Vígi back, I figure it's time to give her a better life and settle down."

While everyone else had started celebrating the new arrangement, Sera found a quiet spot and pulled out the Infinity Ring.

"Whoa, whoa, whoa," Dak said, holding up his hands and stepping out of reach. "Not so fast! Rollo's becoming a duke tomorrow and invited us to the ceremony. That's something I'm *not* going to miss."

Sera rolled her eyes. "We're not warping through time just so we can attend a few parties. There's a Cataclysm we're supposed to be preventing, if you'll recall."

"I don't see why we can't do both," Dak offered, raising his eyebrows and giving her a hopeful smile.

"Are you forgetting that there are Time Wardens after us? They know what we look like, too," she countered.

"We'll wear disguises!" Dak suggested. "It's been a rough few days. Think of this as a morale booster!"

Sera glanced at Riq, who shrugged. "Fine," she finally said. "We stay for the ceremony and then we go. But Dak's in charge of finding us all costumes."

Dak started dancing around the clearing in celebration — it wasn't a pretty sight.

Dak couldn't stop hopping from foot to foot. He hadn't been this excited since he'd unearthed that cache of rare coins from a hidden drawer in a famous antique desk (it wasn't his fault the museum had such poor security). "Can you believe we're actually here for this?" he whispered to Sera for the twenty millionth time.

She glared at him from under a large drooping hat and a tangle of horsehair meant to look like a wig. Her clothes were bulky and dirty, giving her a sloppy, mis-shapen appearance that wasn't helped by the smell. She didn't look pleased, but Dak figured that the worse they smelled, the less likely people would spend enough time around them to realize who they were under the disguises.

He gave her an innocent look in return. She'd put him in charge of procuring disguises; she should have known what she was getting herself into.

Even her discomfort couldn't dull the excitement thrumming through him. It was just all so . . . real! The king's men had been working all day to craft a throne and a dais for the ceremony to take place on. A crowd had started gathering early but Dak had dragged Sera and Riq to the location just beyond the river before the sun rose.

He wasn't going to miss a minute of this!

The procession began with the blaring of horns and the arrival of important guests from nearby villages and towns. Rollo's men were peppered through the crowd, an odd mix of those who, not too long ago, had been fighting against one another tooth and nail.

Speeches were made, descriptions of land and boundaries rattled off, and as the ceremony proceeded, something began to seem amiss to Dak. There were moments when he felt like someone was staring at him but when he glanced through the crowd to find out who it was, there was no one looking in his direction.

The uncomfortable sensation grew as the long day dragged and it began to feel like a weight on his shoulders. He found his mind wandering, his focus diverted from the details of what was going on around him.

On the stage a minstrel was singing a ballad, but Dak's attention was drawn to a group of men gathering on the far edge of the crowd near a copse of trees. They were growing rowdy and something about it piqued Dak's interest.

"Be right back," he murmured to Sera, and before she could say anything to stop him, he'd slipped through the

throng and disappeared. He had to fight against the surg-
ing crowd, everyone pressing forward for a view of the
dais as speculation that the king's arrival was imminent
drifted from mouth to mouth.

Dak kept his gaze focused on the crowd growing
around the disturbance, forcing his way nearer. As he
approached the commotion his heart started to pound
faster, his stomach twisting with an anticipation he didn't
understand.

The mob had their hands raised, shouting out curses.
Dak asked the closest Frank what was going on. "The
devil's spawn, that's what they are," the man hissed before
turning and shouting that they should burn the pair.

He heard a woman cry out, "No!" and then someone
else, a man, shout, "Leave her alone. Get back!"

His blood froze. He knew those voices.

"Mom! Dad!" he yelled, elbowing people out of the
way as he battled his way forward. It was slow going, the
crowd packed so tight that he had to resort to crawling
between legs at times, not caring when someone's heel
crunched his fingers.

All around him people surged, their faces twisted
with rage. Dak had forgotten how superstitious most
people were during this time period. Science as he knew
it didn't exist yet — anything unexplainable was chalked
up to magic.

As he drew closer he caught glimpses of his parents. They both brandished what looked like rifles from
the American Revolutionary War. And rifles wouldn't

be invented until the nineteenth century. No wonder the crowd was going nuts!

"Hold on!" he shouted, shoving two people out of the way. "I'm coming!"

Just as he reached the center of the circle, his parents flickered like a TV channel losing reception. "Wait!" Dak cried out.

His mother stretched out her hand and Dak reached for it. When he closed his fingers it was around nothing but air.

Dak's parents had been pulled out of time. They were gone.

30

Left Hanging

ONCE AGAIN Dak was missing. "Where is he?" Sera hissed at Riq. She felt like she should have this question printed up on a placard so she could just wave it around whenever necessary.

Riq scanned the crowd halfheartedly before turning his attention back to the dais where a man read the terms of the Treaty of Sainte-Clair-sur-Epte. Rollo and the king had finally taken their positions. "I'm sure he just went off to find a better view."

"But I don't see him." She pressed her hand against the Infinity Ring tucked under her bulky cloak. Throughout the day she'd caught glimpses of Gorm wandering through the crowd, and he wasn't alone this time. It was making her anxious.

"The ceremony's started and it's not like him to miss it. Maybe I should go look for him." She'd just started pushing her way through the crowd when she heard a rumble of an argument followed by a collective gasp from those around her.

She spun toward Riq. "What happened?"

He looked stunned, which was unusual for him. "The bishop said that Rollo should kiss the king's foot as a demonstration of his fealty and a thanks for the gift of the land." He turned to face Sera. "Rollo said he'd never bend his knee to anyone or kiss anyone's foot. If he refuses, the ceremony will end without him being appointed the Duke of Normandy."

Sera started feeling slightly panicked. They were so close to fixing this Break — they couldn't let it all fall apart *now*.

"We can still fix this, right?" Riq said.

Sera nodded, slowly. "I think so, if we hurry. But figuring out what it would take —" Riq was already on his feet and pushing through the crowd before Sera could finish the thought.

She stood, trying to follow, but the gaps Riq created in the crush of people closed too fast, and she was brought up short again and again. From her left she heard someone shout and a man with an SQ insignia stitched in his collar began to force his way forward. He pointed directly at her and called for backup.

They were so busted. Again.

Sera swallowed her alarm and concentrated on her efforts at catching Riq. She made it to the front of the crowd, but was too late. He'd already leapt up the steps to the dais and was beyond her reach.

"Riq," she hissed but he couldn't hear and she didn't dare risk drawing more attention to herself. The Infinity

Ring was already preprogrammed for Washington, DC. All she had to do was find Dak and grab Riq, and they could get out of here before being nabbed by the SQ.

Totally easy, she thought, rolling her eyes.

Riq didn't even appear to hesitate as he strode across the dais to where Rollo towered over the king, both of them gesturing heatedly. Sera caught snippets of the argument: The king's bishops demanded Rollo show fealty; Rollo flat-out refused to humiliate himself by kissing another man's muddy boot.

When he spoke, Riq's voice rang clearly over the crowd, silencing everyone. "We can agree that the king wishes for Rollo to occupy around the city of Rouen stretching to the sea, including the mouth of the Seine River, correct?"

Shouts of agreement came from the Vikings in the crowd.

"And we can also agree that in exchange for such generosity, Rollo shall give fealty to the king and defend Francia's borders, can we not?"

This time the Franks in the audience cheered their approval.

Riq knew what he was doing. This crowd was not going to be happy if the treaty fell through — and now both Rollo and King Charles knew it.

"In fact," Riq continued, turning to the two leaders, "a treaty to such effect has already been agreed to, correct?"

After a slight hesitation, both men nodded.

"What's he doing?" someone muttered in a familiar voice and Sera scoured the crowd until she found Dak standing on the other side of the aisle leading to the platform.

They'd strung chains from posts to keep the crowds at bay and there was no way Sera could cross to Dak without drawing a whole lot of unwanted attention.

"Where have you been?" she demanded loud enough that a few surrounding men grumbled for her to be quiet. She noticed that Dak's eyes seemed a bit wild, his body almost vibrating with tension.

She had no idea what would cause him to be so agitated, and she was afraid to find out. Over his shoulder, deeper in the sea of people, Sera saw a pair of SQ agents pushing their way toward the dais. She pointed them out to Dak and he ducked, slipping through a few people to better hide himself. Sera did the same.

Whatever Riq was planning, he'd better hurry up or they'd all be in big trouble.

Riq continued with his speech. "All that remain are the formalities, and I think that both parties can agree to assign such duties to those trusted men among their ranks, right?"

If the king was unhappy with the idea, he didn't show it. Once Rollo gave his assent the king followed suit.

With the flourish of someone who'd obviously spent a lot of time on a stage learning how to woo a crowd, Riq turned to Rollo. "May I have the great honor of representing you for such an honorable act?"

Rollo frowned and shrugged. Riq turned back to the king. "And will you acccpt my substitution on this fine Viking chieftain's behalf?"

The king looked toward his men, clearly lost as to what was going on. Sera had to press her hands to her mouth to keep from giggling. Even though it was clear to her that Riq was overdoing this, the crowd was eating it up.

Eventually the king waved his hand ambiguously. If he'd been expecting Riq to kneel and lower his head to the ground, he was wrong. Riq stepped toward him and took the king's muddy boot firmly in his hand. He then raised it to his mouth without bending over and, with loud exaggeration, kissed it.

Clearly the king was not flexible enough to have his leg lifted so high, and he tumbled backward and off the dais.

Riq turned and beamed. "The king's foot has been kissed and Rollo's fealty given."

The crowd gasped. There was silence. And then someone snorted. Somewhere else there was a stifled giggle, a cough, and before long the entire crowd was roaring with laughter.

The king's attendants helped him to his feet, and Sera saw a flurry of emotions cross his face — bewilderment and frustration at first, but he softened at seeing the amusement of the crowd. The king smiled, apparently deciding that he needed to look like he was in on the joke.

Sera was so caught up in the moment that she wasn't prepared for the hand that clamped on her shoulder and the voice shouting, "Hey, you!"

Sera jumped and screamed, the sound lost in the noise from the crowd. The SQ agent shifted his hand from her squirming shoulder to a long shank of her fake hair. "You're not getting away again," he threatened.

She grinned, stepping sideways and out from under the horsehair wig. "That's what you think!"

Without a second thought, she ducked under the chain blocking the aisle and raced toward Dak, grabbing him and pulling him to where Riq stood on the stage, surrounded by a band of cheerful Vikings.

"The SQ is onto us," she yelled to him over the noise of the crowd. "We have to get out of here!"

Rollo must have seen the urgency on her face and known what it meant, because once the two of them had climbed the stairs and joined Riq, he and his men closed rank around them, facing outward with their weapons drawn.

"Yo, Riq," Dak said, holding out his fist for the older boy to bump it. "That was pretty awesome what you did with the king!"

Riq grinned, obviously pleased by the compliment, and returned the gesture.

"My time-traveling friends, you're leaving so soon?" Rollo asked. Beside him, Vígi whined, her forehead furrowed.

Dak scratched at her ears. "I'm afraid so," he told the

new Duke of Normandy. "Though this time I think we'll leave this lady at home."

Rollo clamped his hand on Dak's shoulder. "You're a strong warrior, smart and true. Thank you for the gift you've given me. I will keep the SQ—whether Frank or Viking—out of Normandy for all time. And I promise to turn away from pillaging and do well by my station as duke. Mostly."

Dak's face blazed bright red at the compliment, but Sera knew he was loving every minute of it. She pulled the Infinity Ring out and started double-checking that everything was set correctly. The last thing she wanted to do was let a last-minute miscalculation send them zooming too far ahead in the future or drop them into the middle of another war zone.

Beside her, someone cleared his throat and she looked up to find Bill. "So that's it, then?"

Sera hesitated and then nodded.

He cleared his throat. "I ran out of time, back in Paris, before I could give you this. I'd meant to, then, and I've held on to it . . . just in case."

He pulled a length of fine chain over his head and held it out to her. A gold charm dangled from the end and she reached out to cup it. It was a tiny infinity symbol, delicate and smoothly polished. "My ancestors were goldsmiths and they passed down the skills."

Sera felt her throat tighten. "Thank you," she whispered.

"I wanted to thank *you*, actually," he said.

That took Sera by surprise. "For what?"

"For being brave," he explained. "I'd have never done anything big in my life, taken any risks, if I hadn't learned that from you."

Sera sputtered, "I'm not really that brave and I hate risks."

In response, Bill smiled. "Maybe you don't see it yet, but I do."

Just then Riq stepped forward and linked his arm with hers. "Our work here is done," Riq announced. "On to 1814!"

"One War of 1812, coming up!" Dak placed his hand on her shoulder after kneeling to allow Vígi to give him one last slobbery kiss.

Sera took a final look around her and smiled at Bill as she pushed the button to send them swirling through time. The Infinity Ring began to vibrate, the scene around her blurring. Her body felt small and impossibly big at the same time. "One more thing," Dak whispered just as everything began to shatter apart. "I saw my parents. They were here and then they warped out in front of my eyes. But not before they left me *this*."

The last thing Sera saw as medieval France disappeared was Dak holding out a large iron key.

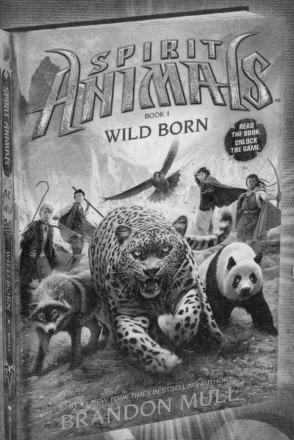